FREN

An Inspector Calls

A Play in Three Acts

Herausgegeben von
Berthold Sturm

Reclam

Diese Ausgabe darf nur in der Bundesrepublik Deutschland, in Österreich und in der Schweiz vertrieben werden.

This edition may only be sold in Germany, Austria and Switzerland

RECLAMS UNIVERSAL-BIBLIOTHEK Nr. 9218

Gesamtherstellung: Reclam, Ditzingen. Printed in Germany 2016
RECLAM, UNIVERSAL-BIBLIOTHEK und RECLAMS UNIVERSAL-BIBLIOTHEK sind eingetragene Marken der Philipp Reclam jun. GmbH & Co. KG, Stuttgart
ISBN 978-3-15-009218-7

www.reclam.de

An Inspector Calls

TO MICHAEL MACOWAN

Characters

ARTHUR BIRLING

SYBIL BIRLING

SHEILA BIRLING

ERIC BIRLING

GERALD CROFT

EDNA

INSPECTOR GOOLE

Acts

All three acts, which are continuous, take place in the dining-room of the Birlings' house in Brumley, an industrial city in the North Midlands. It is an evening in spring, 1912.

Act I

The dining-room of a fairly large suburban house, belonging to a prosperous manufacturer. It has good solid furniture of the period. The general effect is substantial and heavily comfortable, but not cosy and homelike. (If a realistic set is used, then it should be swung back, as it was in the Old Vic production at the New Theatre.[1] *By doing this, you can have the dining-table centre downstage during Act I, when it is needed there, and then, swinging back, can reveal the fireplace for Act II, and then for Act III can show a small table with telephone on it, downstage of fireplace; and by this time the dining-table and its chairs have moved well upstage. Producers who wish to avoid this tricky business, which involves two re-settings of the scene and some very accurate adjustments of the extra flats necessary, would be well advised to dispense with an ordinary realistic set, if only because the dining-table becomes a nuisance. The lighting should be pink and intimate until*

2 **suburban:** vorstädtisch.
4 **substantial:** solide.
5 **cosy:** behaglich.
6 **set:** Bühnenbild.
8 **downstage:** im Bühnenvordergrund.
13 **upstage:** im Bühnenhintergrund.
producer: Regisseur.
14 **re-settings:** Umbauten.
15 **adjustment:** Anpassung.
flat: Kulisse.
16 **to dispense with s.th.:** ohne etwas fertig werden, auskommen.
18 **nuisance:** Störfaktor, Ärgernis.

the Inspector arrives, and then it should be brighter and harder.)

At rise of curtain, the four Birlings and Gerald are seated at the table, with Arthur Birling at one end, his wife at the other, Eric downstage, and Sheila and Gerald seated upstage. Edna, the parlour-maid, is just clearing the table, which has no cloth, of dessert plates and champagne glasses, etc., and then replacing them with decanter of port, cigar box and cigarettes. Port glasses are already on the table. All five are in evening dress of the period, the men in tails and white ties, not dinner-jackets. Arthur Birling is a heavy-looking, rather portentous man in his middle fifties with fairly easy manners but rather provincial in his speech. His wife is about fifty, a rather cold woman and her husband's social superior. Sheila is a pretty girl in her early twenties, very pleased with life and rather excited. Gerald Croft is an attractive chap about thirty, rather too manly to be a dandy but very much the easy well-bred young man-about-town. Eric is in his early twenties, not quite at ease, half shy, half assertive. At the moment they

6 **parlour-maid:** Dienstmädchen.
7 **dessert:** Nachtisch.
8 **decanter:** Karaffe.
port: Portwein.
11 **tails** (pl., coll.): Frack.
dinner-jacket: Dinnerjacket (Herrenjackett für formelle gesellschaftliche Anlässe).
12 **portentous:** gewaltig, ungeheuer.
13 **easy manners:** zwanglose Manieren.
17 **chap** (coll.): Bursche.
18 **dandy:** Geck, Stutzer.
well-bred: wohlerzogen.
19 **man-about-town:** Lebemann, Salonlöwe.
20 **to be at ease:** sich wohl fühlen.
assertive: anmaßend; geltungsbedürftig.

have all had a good dinner, are celebrating a special occasion, and are pleased with themselves.

BIRLING. Giving us the port, Edna? That's right. *(He pushes it towards Eric.)* You ought to like this port, Gerald. As a matter of fact, Finchley told me it's exactly the same port your father gets from him.

GERALD. The it'll be all rigth. The governor prides himself on being a good judge of port. I don't pretend to know moch about it.

SHEILA *(gaily, possessively)*. I should jolly well think not, Gerald. I'd hate you to know all about port – like one of these purple-faced old men.

BIRLING. Here, I'm not a purple-faced old man.

SHEILA. No, not yet. But then you don't know all about port – do you?

BIRLING *(noticing that his wife has not taken any)*. Now then, Sybil, you must take a little to-night. Special occasion, y'know, eh?

SHEILA. Yes, go on, Mummy. You must drink our health.

MRS. BIRLING *(smiling)*. Very well, then. Just a little, thank you. *(To Edna, who is about to go, with tray.)* All right, Edna. I'll ring from the drawing-room when we want coffee. Probably in about half an hour.

EDNA *(going)*. Yes, ma'am.

(Edna goes out. They now have all the glasses filled. Birling beams at them and clearly relaxes.)

7 **governor** (coll.): alter Herr, Vater.
7 f. **to pride o.s. on s.th.:** sich etwas auf eine Sache einbilden.
10 **possessively** (adv.): besitzergreifend, vereinnahmend.
jolly (adv., coll.): sehr, ziemlich.
18 **y'know** (coll.): *you know:* nicht wahr?
26 **to relax:** sich entspannen.

BIRLING. Well, well – this is very nice. Very nice. Good dinner too, Sybil. Tell cook from me.

GERALD *(politely)*. Absolutely first-class.

MRS. BIRLING *(reproachfully)*. Arthur, you're not supposed to say such things —

BIRLING. Oh – come, come – I'm treating Gerald like one of the family. And I'm sure he won't object.

SHEILA *(with mock aggressiveness)*. Go on, Gerald – just you object!

GERALD *(smiling)*. Wouldn't dream of it. In fact, I insist upon being one of the family now. I've been trying long enough, haven't I? *(As she does not reply, with more insistence.)* Haven't I? You know I have.

MRS. BIRLING *(smiling)*. Of course she does.

SHEILA *(half serious, half playful)*. Yes – except for all last summer, when you never came near me, and I wondered what had happened to you.

GERALD. And I've told you – I was awfully busy at the works all that time.

SHEILA *(same tone as before)*. Yes, that's what *you* say.

MRS. BIRLING. Now, Sheila, don't tease him. When you're married you'll realise that men with important work to do sometimes have to spend nearly all their time and energy on their business. You'll have to get used to that, just as I had.

SHEILA. I don't believe I will. *(Half playful, half serious, to Gerald.)* So you be careful.

GERALD. Oh – I will, I will.

4 **reproachfully** (adv.): vorwurfsvoll.
8 **mock:** gespielt, Schein-, Pseudo-.
13 **insistence:** Nachdruck.
21 **to tease:** necken.

(Eric suddenly guffaws. His parents look at him.)

SHEILA *(severely)*. Now – what's the joke?

ERIC. I don't know – really. Suddenly I felt I just had to laugh.

SHEILA. You're squiffy.

ERIC. I'm not.

MRS. BIRLING. What an expression, Sheila! Really, the things you girls pick up these days!

ERIC. If you think that's the best she can do —

SHEILA. Don't be an ass, Eric.

MRS. BIRLING. Now stop it, you two. Arthur, what about this famous toast of yours?

BIRLING. Yes, of course. *(Clears his throat.)* Well, Gerald, I know you agreed that we should only have this quiet little family party. It's a pity Sir George – and – er – Lady Croft can't be with us, but they're abroad and so it can't be helped. As I told you, they sent me a very nice cable – couldn't be nicer. I'm not sorry that we're celebrating quietly like this —

MRS. BIRLING. Much nicer really.

GERALD. I agree.

BIRLING. So do I, but it makes speech-making more difficult —

ERIC *(not too rudely)*. Well, don't do any. We'll drink their health and have done with it.

BIRLING. No, we won't. It's one of the happiest nights of my life. And one day, I hope, Eric, when you've a daughter of your own, you'll understand why. Gerald,

1 **to guffaw:** schallend lachen.
5 **squiffy** (coll.): angesäuselt, beschwipst.
10 **ass:** (fig.) Esel, Dummkopf.
24 **rudely** (adv.): grob, rüde.

I'm going to tell you frankly, without any pretences, that your engagement to Sheila means a tremendous lot to me. She'll make you happy, and I'm sure you'll make her happy. You're just the kind of son-in-law I always wanted. Your father and I have been friendly rivals in business for some time now – though Crofts Limited are both older and bigger than Birling and Company – and now you've brought us together, and perhaps we may look forward to the time when Crofts and Birlings are no longer competing but are working together – for lower costs and higher prices.

GERALD. Hear, hear! And I think my father would agree to that.

MRS. BIRLING. Now, Arthur, I don't think you ought to talk business on an occasion like this.

SHEILA. Neither do I. All wrong.

BIRLING. Quite so, I agree with you. I only mentioned it in passing. What I did want to say was – that Sheila's a lucky girl – and I think you're a pretty fortunate young man too, Gerald.

GERALD. I know I am – this once anyhow.

BIRLING *(raising his glass)*. So here's wishing the pair of you – the very best that life can bring. Gerald and Sheila.

MRS. BIRLING *(raising her glass, smiling)*. Yes, Gerald. Yes, Sheila darling. Our congratulations and very best wishes!

GERALD. Thank you.

MRS. BIRLING. Eric!

1 **pretence:** Verstellung; Vorwand.
7 **Limited:** Gesellschaft mit beschränkter Haftung.

ERIC *(rather noisily)*. All the best! She's got a nasty temper sometimes – but she's not bad really. Good old Sheila!

SHEILA. Chump! I can't drink to this, can I? When do I drink?

GERALD. You can drink to me.

SHEILA *(quiet and serious now)*. All right then. I drink to you, Gerald.

(For a moment they look at each other.)

GERALD *(quietly)*. Thank you. And I drink to you – and hope I can make you as happy as you deserve to be.

SHEILA *(trying to be light and easy)*. You be careful – or I'll start weeping.

GERALD *(smiling)*. Well, perhaps this will help to stop it.

(He produces a ring case.)

SHEILA *(excited)*. Oh – Gerald – you've got it – is it the one you wanted me to have?

GERALD *(giving the case to her)*. Yes – the very one.

SHEILA *(taking out the ring)*. Oh – it's wonderful! Look – Mummy – isn't it a beauty? Oh – darling – *(She kisses Gerald hastily.)*

ERIC. Steady the Buffs![2]

SHEILA *(who has put ring on, admiringly)*. I think it's perfect. Now I really feel engaged.

MRS. BIRLING. So you ought, darling. It's a lovely ring. Be careful with it.

SHEILA. Careful! I'll never let it go out of my sight for an instant.

MRS. BIRLING *(smiling)*. Well, it came just at the right

1 **nasty:** garstig, übel, schlimm, böse.
4 **chump** (coll.): Trottel, Dummkopf.
22 **Steady the Buffs!:** etwa: Ruhig Blut!

moment. That was clever of you, Gerald. Now, Arthur, if you've no more to say, I think Sheila and I had better go into the drawing-room and leave you men –

BIRLING *(rather heavily)*. I just want to say this. *(Noticing that Sheila is still admiring her ring.)* Are you listening, Sheila? This concerns you too. And after all I don't often make speeches at you —

SHEILA. I'm sorry, Daddy. Actually I was listening.

(She looks attentive, as they all do. He holds them for a moment before continuing.)

BIRLING. I'm delighted about this engagement and I hope it won't be too long before you're married. And I want to say this. There's a good deal of silly talk about these days – *but* – and I speak as a hard-headed business man, who has to take risks and know what he's about – I say, you can ignore all this silly pessimistic talk. When you marry, you'll be marrying at a very good time. Yes, a very good time – and soon it'll be an even better time. Last month, just because the miners came out on strike, there's a lot of wild talk about possible labour trouble in the near future. Don't worry. We've passed the worst of it. We employers at last are coming together to see that our interests – and the interests of Capital – are properly protected. And we're in for a time of steadily increasing prosperity.

GERALD. I believe you're right, sir.

ERIC. What about war?

BIRLING. Glad you mentioned it, Eric. I'm coming to that.

10 **attentive:** aufmerksam.
to hold s.o.: jdn. in Spannung halten.
15 **hard-headed:** realistisch.
25 **to be in for s.th.:** etwas zu erwarten haben.

Just because the Kaiser[3] makes a speech or two, or a few German officers have too much to drink and begin talking nonsense, you'll hear some people say that war's inevitable. And to that I say – fiddlesticks! The Germans don't want war. Nobody wants war, except some half-civilised folks in the Balkans. And why? There's too much at stake these days. Everything to lose and nothing to gain by war.

ERIC. Yes, I know – but still —

BIRLING. Just let me finish, Eric. You've a lot to learn yet. And I'm talking as a hard-headed, practical man of business. And I say there isn't a chance of war. The world's developing so fast that it'll make war impossible. Look at the progress we're making. In a year or two we'll have aeroplanes that will be able to go anywhere. And look at the way the automobile's making headway – bigger and faster all the time. And then ships. Why, a friend of mine went over this new liner last week – the *Titanic*[4] – she sails next week – forty-six thousand eight hundred tons – forty-six thousand eight hundred tons – New York in five days – and every luxury – and unsinkable, absolutely unsinkable. That's what you've got to keep your eye on, facts like that, progress like that – and not a few German officers talking nonsense and a few scaremongers here making a fuss about nothing. Now you three young people,

4 **inevitable:** unvermeidlich.
fiddlesticks (pl.): Unsinn!
6 **Balkans:** Balkan(staaten).
7 **to be at stake:** auf dem Spiel stehen.
16 f. **to make headway:** Fortschritte machen.
18 **liner:** Linienschiff.
25 **scaremonger:** Panikmacher.
25 f. **to make a fuss about s.th.:** viel Lärm um etwas machen.

just listen to this – and remember what I'm telling you now. In twenty or thirty years' time – let's say, in 1940 – you may be giving a little party like this – your son or daughter might be getting engaged – and I tell you by that time you'll be living in a world that'll have forgotten all these Capital versus Labour[5] agitations and all these silly little war scares. There'll be peace and prosperity and rapid progress everywhere – except of course in Russia, which will always be behindhand, naturally.

MRS. BIRLING. Arthur!

(As Mrs. Birling shows signs of interrupting.)

BIRLING. Yes, my dear, I know – I'm talking too much. But you youngsters just remember what I said. We can't let these Bernard Shaws and H. G. Wellses[6] do all the talking. We hard-headed practical business men must say something sometime. And we don't guess – we've had experience – and we *know*.

MRS. BIRLING *(rising. The others rise)*. Yes, of course, dear. Well – don't keep Gerald in here too long. Eric – I want you a minute.

(She and Sheila and Eric go out. Birling and Gerald sit down again.)

BIRLING. Cigar?

GERALD. No, thanks. Can't really enjoy them.

BIRLING *(taking one himself)*. Ah, you don't know what you're missing. I like a good cigar. *(Indicating decanter.)* Help yourself.

6 **versus** (lat.): gegen.
7 **scare:** Panik, Schrecken.
9 **behindhand:** rückständig.
14 **youngster:** junger Bursche.

GERALD. Thank you.

(Birling lilghts his cigar and Gerald, who has lit a cigarette, helps himself to port then pushes decanter to Birling.)

BIRLING. Thanks. *(Confidentially.)* By the way, there's something I'd like to mention – in strict confidence – while we're by ourselves. I have an idea that your mother – Lady Croft – while she doesn't object to my girl – feels you might have done better for yourself socially —

(Gerald, rather embarrassed, begins to murmur some dissent, but Birling checks him.)

No, Gerald, that's all right. Don't blame her. She comes from an old county family – landed people and so forth – and so it's only natural. But what I wanted to say is – there's a fair chance that I might find my way into the next Honours List.[7] Just a knighthood, of course.

GERALD. Oh – I say – congratulations!

BIRLING. Thanks. But it's a bit too early for that. So don't say anything. But I've had a hint or two. You see, I was Lord Mayor here two years ago when Royalty visited us. And I've always been regarded as a sound useful party man. So – well – I gather there's a very good chance of a knighthood – so long as we behave ourselves, don't get into the police court or start a scandal – eh? *(Laughs complacently.)*

11 **embarrassed:** verlegen.
12 **dissent:** abweichende Meinung.
17 **knighthood:** Ritterwürde.
23 **sound:** zuverlässig.
27 **complacently** (adv.): selbstzufrieden.

GERALD *(laughs)*. You seem to be a nice well-behaved family —

BIRLING. We think we are —

GERALD. So if that's the only obstacle, sir, I think you might as well accept my congratulations now.

BIRLING. No, no, I couldn't do that. And don't say anything yet.

GERALD. Not even to my mother? I know she'd be delighted.

BIRLING. Well, when she comes back, you might drop a hint to her. And you can promise her that we'll try to keep out of trouble during the next few months. *(They both laugh. Eric enters.)*

ERIC. What's the joke? Started telling stories?

BIRLING. No. Want another glass of port?

ERIC *(sitting down)*. Yes, please. *(Takes decanter and helps himself.)* Mother says we mustn't stay too long. But I don't think it matters. I left 'em talking about clothes again. You'd think a girl had never had any clothes before she gets married. Women are potty about 'em.

BIRLING. Yes, but you've got to remember, my boy, that clothes mean something quite different to a woman. Not just something to wear – and not only something to make 'em look prettier – but – well, a sort of sign or token of their self-respect.

GERALD. That's true.

ERIC *(eagerly)*. Yes, I remember — *(but he checks himself.)*

4 **obstacle:** Hindernis.
20 f. **to be potty about s.th.** (coll.): nach etwas verrückt sein.
26 **token:** Zeichen.

BIRLING. Well, what do you remember?

ERIC *(confused)*. Nothing.

BIRLING. Nothing?

GERALD *(amused)*. Sounds a bit fishy to me.

BIRLING *(taking it in same manner)*. Yes, you don't know what some of these boys get up to nowadays. More money to spend and time to spare than I had when I was Eric's age. They worked us hard in those days and kept us short of cash. Though even then – we broke out and had a bit of fun sometimes.

GERALD. I'll bet you did.

BIRLING *(solemnly)*. But this is the point. I don't want to lecture you two young fellows again. But what so many of you don't seem to understand now, when things are so much easier, is that a man has to make his own way – has to look after himself – and his family too, of course, when he has one – and so long as he does that he won't come to much harm. But the way some of these cranks talk and write now, you'd think everybody has to look after everybody else, as if we were all mixed up together like bees in a hive – community and all that nonsense. But take my word for it, you youngsters – and I've learnt in the good hard school of experience – that a man has to mind his own business and look after himself and his own – and —

(We hear the sharp ring of a front door bell. Birling stops to listen.)

ERIC. Somebody at the front door.

4 **fishy** (coll.): verdächtig.
6 **to get up to s.th.:** etwas erreichen, zustandebringen.
19 **crank** (coll.): Spinner, komischer Kauz.
21 **hive:** Bienenstock, Bienenkorb.

BIRLING. Edna'll answer it. Well, have another glass of port, Gerald – and then we'll join the ladies. That'll stop me giving you good advice.

ERIC. Yes, you've piled it on a bit to-night, Father.

BIRLING. Special occasion. And feeling contented, for once, I wanted you to have the benefit of my experience.

(Edna enters.)

EDNA. Please, sir, an inspector's called.

BIRLING. An inspector? What kind of inspector?

EDNA. A police inspector. He says his name's Inspector Goole.

BIRLING. Don't know him. Does he want to see me?

EDNA. Yes, sir. He says it's important.

BIRLING. All right, Edna. Show him in here. Give us some more light.

(Edna does, then goes out.)

I'm still on the Bench. It may be something about a warrant.

GERALD *(lightly)*. Sure to be. Unless Eric's been up to something. *(Nodding confidentially to Birling.)* And that would be awkward, wouldn't it?

BIRLING *(humorously)*. Very.

ERIC *(who is uneasy, sharply)*. Here, what do you mean?

GERALD *(lightly)*. Only something we were talking about when you were out. A joke really.

ERIC *(still uneasy)*. Well, I don't think it's very funny.

BIRLING *(sharply, staring at him)*. What's the matter with *you?*

18 **to be on the Bench** (jur.): (Laien-)Richter sein.
19 **warrant:** richterliche Verfügung (z. B. Haftbefehl); Vollmacht.
22 **awkward:** peinlich.

ERIC *(defiantly)*. Nothing.

EDNA *(opening door, and announcing)*. Inspector Goole. *(The Inspector enters, and Edna goes, closing door after her. The Inspector need not be a big man but he creates at once an impression of massiveness, solidity and purposefulness. He is a man in his fifties, dressed in a plain darkish suit of the period. He speaks carefully, weightily, and has a disconcerting habit of looking hard at the person he addresses before actually speaking.)*

INSPECTOR. Mr. Birling?

BIRLING. Yes. Sit down, Inspector.

INSPECTOR *(sitting)*. Thank you, sir.

BIRLING. Have a glass of port – or a little whisky?

INSPECTOR. No, thank you, Mr. Birling. I'm on duty.

BIRLING. You're new, aren't you?

INSPECTOR. Yes, sir. Only recently transferred.

BIRLING. I thought you must be. I was an alderman for years – and Lord Mayor two years ago – and I'm still on the Bench – so I know the Brumley police officers pretty well – and I thought I'd never seen you before.

INSPECTOR. Quite so.

BIRLING. Well, what can I do for you? Some trouble about a warrant?

INSPECTOR. No, Mr. Birling.

BIRLING *(after a pause, with a touch of impatience)*. Well, what is it then?

INSPECTOR. I'd like some information, if you don't mind, Mr. Birling. Two hours ago a young woman died in the

1 **defiantly** (adv.): trotzig.
5 **massiveness:** Wucht.
8 **disconcerting:** beunruhigend, verwirrend.
17 **alderman:** Ratsherr.

Infirmary. She'd been taken there this afternoon because she'd swallowed a lot of strong disinfectant. Burnt her inside out, of course.

ERIC *(involuntarily)*. My God!

INSPECTOR. Yes, she was in great agony. They did everything they could for her at the Infirmary, but she died. Suicide of course.

BIRLING *(rather impatiently)*. Yes, yes. Horrible business. But I don't understand why you should come here, Inspector —

INSPECTOR *(cutting through, massively)*. I've been round to the room she had, and she'd left a letter there and a sort of diary. Like a lot of these young women who get into various kinds of trouble, she'd used more than one name. But her original name – her real name – was Eva Smith.

BIRLING *(thoughtfully)*. Eva Smith?

INSPECTOR. Do you remember her, Mr. Birling?

BIRLING *(slowly)*. No – I seem to remember hearing that name – Eva Smith – somewhere. But it doesn't convey anything to me. And I don't see where I come into this.

INSPECTOR. She was employed in your works at one time.

BIRLING. Oh – that's it, is it? Well, we've several hundred young women there, y'know, and they keep changing.

INSPECTOR. This young woman, Eva Smith, was a bit out

1 **infirmary:** Krankenhaus.
2 **disinfectant:** Desinfektionsmittel.
5 **to be in agony:** unter unerträglichen Schmerzen leiden.
7 **suicide:** Selbstmord.
11 **massively** (adv.): (fig.) massiv, fest.
13 **diary:** Tagebuch.
20 **to convey:** besagen.
21 **to come into s.th.:** mit etwas zu tun haben, in etwas verwickelt sein.

of the ordinary. I found a photograph of her in her lodgings. Perhaps you'd remember her from that.

(Inspector takes a photograph, about postcard size, out of his pocket and goes to Birling. Both Gerald and Eric rise to have a look at the photograph, but the Inspector interposes himself between them and the photograph. They are surprised and rather annoyed. Birling stares hard, and with recognition, at the photograph, which the Inspector then replaces in his pocket.)

GERALD *(showing annoyance)*. Any particular reason why I shouldn't see this girl's photograph, Inspector?

INSPECTOR *(coolly, looking hard at him)*. There might be.

ERIC. And the same applies to me, I suppose?

INSPECTOR Yes.

GERALD. I can't imagine what it could be.

ERIC. Neither can I.

BIRLING. And I must say, I agree with them, Inspector.

INSPECTOR. It's the way I like to go to work. One person and one line of enquiry at a time. Otherwise, there's a muddle.

BIRLING. I see. Sensible really. *(Moves restlessly, then turns.)* You've had enough of that port, Eric.

(The Inspector is watching Birling and now Birling notices him.)

INSPECTOR. I think you remember Eva Smith now, don't you, Mr. Birling?

BIRLING. Yes, I do. She was one of my employees and then I discharged her.

2 **lodgings** (pl.): möbliertes Zimmer.
6 **to interpose o.s. between s.th.:** sich zwischen etwas stellen.
20 **muddle:** Durcheinander.
27 **employee:** Arbeitnehmer(in).

ERIC. Is that why she committed suicide? When was this, Father?

BIRLING. Just keep quiet, Eric, and don't get excited. This girl left us nearly two years ago. Let me see – it must have been in the early autumn of nineteen-ten.

INSPECTOR. Yes. End of September, nineteen-ten.

BIRLING. That's right.

GERALD. Look here, sir. Wouldn't you rather I was out of this?

BIRLING. I don't mind your being here, Gerald. And I'm sure you've no objection, have you, Inspector? Perhaps I ought to explain first that this is Mr. Gerald Croft – the son of Sir George Croft – you know, Crofts Limited.

INSPECTOR. Mr. Gerald Croft, eh?

BIRLING. Yes. Incidentally we've been modestly celebrating his engagement to my daughter, Sheila.

INSPECTOR. I see. Mr. Croft is going to marry Miss Sheila Birling.

GERALD *(smiling)*. I hope so.

INSPECTOR *(gravely)*. Then I'd prefer you to stay.

GERALD *(surprised)*. Oh – all right.

BIRLING *(somewhat impatiently)*. Look – there's nothing mysterious – or scandalous – about this business – at least not so far as I'm concerned. It's a perfectly straightforward case, and as it happened more than eighteen months ago – nearly two years ago – obviously it has nothing whatever to do with the wretched girl's suicide. Eh, Inspector?

INSPECTOR. No, sir. I can't agree with you there.

16 **incidentally** (adv.): zufälligerweise.
26 **straightforward:** redlich.

BIRLING. Why not?

INSPECTOR. Because what happened to her then may have determined what happened to her afterwards, and what happened to her afterwards may have driven her to suicide. A chain of events.

BIRLING. Oh well – put like that, there's something in what you say. Still, I can't accept any responsibility. If we were all responsible for everything that happened to everybody we'd had anything to do with, it would be very awkward, wouldn't it?

INSPECTOR. Very awkward.

BIRLING. We'd all be in an impossible position, wouldn't we?

ERIC. By Jove, yes. And as you were saying, Dad, a man has to look after himself —

BIRLING. Yes, well, we needn't go into all that.

INSPECTOR. Go into what?

BIRLING. Oh – just before you came – I'd been giving these young men a little good advice. Now – about this girl, Eva Smith. I remember her quite well now. She was a lively good-looking girl – country-bred, I fancy – and she'd been working in one of our machine shops for over a year. A good worker too. In fact, the foreman there told me he was ready to promote her into what we call a leading operator – head of a small group of girls. But after they came back from their holidays in August, they were all rather restless, and they suddenly decided to ask for more money. They were

14 **by Jove:** bei Gott!
21 **country-bred:** auf dem Lande großgeworden.
22 **machine shop:** Maschinenhalle.
25 **leading operator:** Vorarbeiter(in).

averaging about twenty-two and six, which was neither more nor less than is paid generally in our industry. They wanted the rates raised so that they could average about twenty-five shillings a week. I refused, of course.

INSPECTOR. Why?

BIRLING *(surprised)*. Did you say "Why?"?

INSPECTOR. Yes. Why did you refuse?

BIRLING. Well, Inspector, I don't see that it's any concern of yours how I choose to run my business. Is it now?

INSPECTOR. It might be, you know.

BIRLING. I don't like the tone.

INSPECTOR. I'm sorry. But you asked me a question.

BIRLING. And you asked me a question before that, a quite unnecessary question too.

INSPECTOR. It's my duty to ask questions.

BIRLING. Well, it's my duty to keep labour costs down, and if I'd agreed to this demand for a new rate we'd have added about twelve per cent to our labour costs. Does that satisfy you? So I refused. Said I couldn't consider it. We were paying the usual rates and if they didn't like those rates, they could go and work somewhere else. It's a free country, I told them.

ERIC. It isn't if you can't go and work somewhere else.

INSPECTOR. Quite so.

BIRLING*(to Eric)*. Look – just you keep out of this. You hadn't even started in the works when this happened. So they went on strike. That didn't last long, of course.

GERALD. Not if it was just after the holidays. They'd be all broke – if I know them.

1 **to average:** durchschnittlich haben.
3 **rate:** Lohnquote, Tarif.
30 **broke** (coll.): pleite, abgebrannt.

BIRLING. Right, Gerald. They mostly were. And so was the strike, after a week or two. Pitiful affair. Well, we let them all come back – at the old rates – except the four or five ringleaders, who'd started the trouble. I went down myself and told them to clear out. And this girl, Eva Smith, was one of them. She'd had a lot to say – far too much – so she had to go.

GERALD. You couldn't have done anything else.

ERIC. He could. He could have kept her on instead of throwing her out. I call it tough luck.

BIRLING. Rubbish! If you don't come down sharply on some of these people, they'd soon be asking for the earth.

GERALD. I should say so!

INSPECTOR. They might. But after all it's better to ask for the earth than to take it.

BIRLING *(staring at the Inspector)*. What did you say your name was, Inspector?

INSPECTOR. Goole. G, double O – L – E.

BIRLING. How do you get on with our Chief Constable, Colonel Roberts?

INSPECTOR. I don't see much of him.

BIRLING. Perhaps I ought to warn you that he's an old friend of mine, and that I see him fairly frequently. We play golf together sometimes up at the West Brumley.

INSPECTOR *(dryly)*. I don't play golf.

BIRLING. I didn't suppose you did.

ERIC *(bursting out)*. Well, I think it's a dam' shame.

4 **ringleader:** Anführer, Rädelsführer.
10 **tough luck** (coll.): Pech.
11 **rubbish** (coll.): Unsinn.
to come down sharply on s.o.: jdn. scharf anfassen.
20 **Chief Constable:** Polizeipräsident.
28 **dam':** Kurzform von *damned:* verdammt.

INSPECTOR. No, I've never wanted to play.

ERIC. No. I mean about this girl – Eva Smith. Why shouldn't they try for higher wages? We try for the highest possible prices. And I don't see why she should have been sacked just because she'd a bit more spirit than the others. You said yourself she was a good worker. I'd have let her stay.

BIRLING *(rather angrily)*. Unless you brighten your ideas, you'll never be in a position to let anybody stay or to tell anybody to go. It's about time you learnt to face a few responsibilities. That's something this public-school-and-Varsity life[8] you've had doesn't seem to teach you.

ERIC *(sulkily)*. Well, we don't need to tell the Inspector all about that, do we?

BIRLING. I don't see we need to tell the Inspector anything more. In fact, there's nothing I can tell him. I told the girl to clear out, and she went. That's the last I heard of her. Have you any idea what happened to her after that? Get into trouble? Go on the streets?

INSPECTOR *(rather slowly)*. No, she didn't exactly go on the streets. *(Sheila has now entered.)*

SHEILA *(gaily)*. What's this about streets? *(Noticing the Inspector.)* Oh – sorry. I didn't know. Mummy sent me in to ask you why you didn't come along to the drawing-room.

BIRLING. We shall be along in a minute now. Just finishing.

5 **to sack s.o.** (coll.): jdn. an die Luft setzen.
12 **Varsity** (coll.): Uni(versität).
14 **sulkily** (adv.): schmollend.
20 **to go on the streets:** auf den Strich gehen.

INSPECTOR. I'm afraid not.

BIRLING *(abruptly)*. There's nothing else, y'know. I've just told you that.

SHEILA. What's all this about?

BIRLING. Nothing to do with you, Sheila. Run along.

INSPECTOR. No, wait a minute, Miss Birling.

BIRLING *(angrily)*. Look here, Inspector, I consider this uncalled-for and officious. I've half a mind to report you. I've told you all I know – and it doesn't seem to me very important – and now there isn't the slightest reason why my daughter should be dragged into this unpleasant business.

SHEILA *(coming further in)*. What business? What's happening?

INSPECTOR *(impressively)*. I'm a police inspector, Miss Birling. This afternoon a young woman drank some disinfectant, and died, after several hours of agony, tonight in the Infirmary.

SHEILA. Oh – how horrible! Was it an accident?

INSPECTOR. No. She wanted to end her life. She felt she couldn't go on any longer.

BIRLING. Well, don't tell me that's because I discharged her from my employment nearly two years ago.

ERIC. That might have started it.

SHEILA. Did you, Dad?

BIRLING. Yes. The girl had been causing trouble in the works. I was quite justified.

GERALD. Yes, I think you were. I know we'd have done the same thing. Don't look like that, Sheila.

SHEILA *(rather distressed)*. Sorry! It's just that I can't help

8 **officious:** übertrieben diensteifrig.
30 **distressed:** niedergeschlagen, in Not.

thinking about this girl – destroying herself so horribly – and I've been so happy to-night. Oh I wish you hadn't told me. What was she like? Quite young?

INSPECTOR. Yes. Twenty-four.

SHEILA. Pretty?

INSPECTOR. She wasn't pretty when I saw her to-day, but she had been pretty – very pretty.

BIRLING. That's enough of that.

GERALD. And I don't really see that this enquiry gets you anywhere, Inspector. It's what happened to her since she left Mr. Birling's works that is important.

BIRLING. Obviously. I suggested that some time ago.

GERALD. And we can't help you there because we don't know.

INSPECTOR *(slowly)*. Are you sure you don't know?

(He looks at Gerald, then at Eric, then at Sheila.)

BIRLING. And are you suggesting now that one of them knows something about this girl?

INSPECTOR. Yes.

BIRLING. You didn't come here just to see me then?

INSPECTOR. No.

(The other four exchange bewildered and perturbed glances.)

BIRLING *(with marked change of tone)*. Well, of course, if I'd known that earlier, I wouldn't have called you officious and talked about reporting you. You understand that, don't you, Inspector? I thought that – for some reason best known to yourself – you were making the most of this tiny bit of information I could give you. I'm sorry. This makes a difference. You sure of your facts?

22 **perturbed:** beunruhigt, verstört.

INSPECTOR. Some of them – yes.

BIRLING. I can't think they can be of any great consequence.

INSPECTOR. The girl's dead though.

SHEILA. What do you mean by saying that? You talk as if we were responsible —

BIRLING *(cutting in)*. Just a minute, Sheila. Now, Inspector, perhaps you and I had better go and talk this over quietly in a corner —

SHEILA *(cutting in)*. Why should you? He's finished with you. He says it's one of us now.

BIRLING. Yes, and I'm trying to settle it sensibly for you.

GERALD. Well, there's nothing to settle as far as I'm concerned. I've never known an Eva Smith.

ERIC. Neither have I.

SHEILA. Was that her name? Eva Smith?

GERALD. Yes.

SHEILA. Never heard it before.

GERALD. So where are you now, Inspector?

INSPECTOR. Where I was before, Mr. Croft. I told you – that like a lot of these young women, she'd used more than one name. She was still Eva Smith when Mr. Birling sacked her – for wanting twenty-five shillings a week instead of twenty-two and six. But after that she stopped being Eva Smith. Perhaps she'd had enough of it.

ERIC. Can't blame her.

SHEILA *(to Birling)*. I think it was a mean thing to do. Perhaps that spoilt everything for her.

BIRLING. Rubbish! *(To Inspector.)* Do you know what happened to this girl after she left my works?

2 f. **consequence:** Bedeutung.

INSPECTOR. Yes. She was out of work for the next two months. Both her parents were dead, so that she'd no home to go back to. And she hadn't been able to save much out of what Birling and Company had paid her. So that after two months, with no work, no money coming in, and living in lodgings, with no relatives to help her, few friends, lonely, half-starved, she was feeling desperate.

SHEILA *(warmly)*. I should think so. It's a rotten shame.

INSPECTOR. There are a lot of young women living that sort of existence in every city and big town in this country, Miss Birling. If there weren't, the factories and warehouses wouldn't know where to look for cheap labour. Ask your father.

SHEILA. But these girls aren't cheap labour – they're *people*.

INSPECTOR *(dryly)*. I've had that notion myself from time to time. In fact, I've thought that it would do us all a bit of good if sometimes we tried to put ourselves in the place of these young women counting their pennies in their dingy little back bedrooms.

SHEILA. Yes, I expect it would. But what happened to her then?

INSPECTOR. She had what seemed to her a wonderful stroke of luck. She was taken on in a shop – and a good shop too – Milwards.

SHEILA. Milwards! We go there – in fact, I was there this afternoon — *(archly to Gerald)* for *your* benefit.

9 **rotten** (slang): hundsmiserabel, saumäßig.
13 **warehouse:** Lagerhaus.
21 **dingy:** schmutzig, schäbig.
25 **stroke of luck:** Glückstreffer.
28 **archly** (adv.): schelmisch.

GERALD *(smiling)*. Good!

SHEILA. Yes, she was lucky to get taken on at Milwards.

INSPECTOR. That's what she thought. And it happened that at the beginning of December that year – nineteen-ten – there was a good deal of influenza about, and Milwards suddenly found themselves short-handed. So that gave her her chance. It seems she liked working there. It was a nice change from a factory. She enjoyed being among pretty clothes, I've no doubt. And now she felt she was making a good fresh start. You can imagine how she felt.

SHEILA. Yes, of course.

BIRLING. And then she got herself into trouble there, I suppose?

INSPECTOR. After about a couple of months, just when she felt she was settling down nicely, they told her she'd have to go.

BIRLING. Not doing her work properly?

INSPECTOR. There was nothing wrong with the way she was doing her work. They admitted that.

BIRLING. There must have been something wrong.

INSPECTOR. All she knew was – that a customer complained about her – and so she had to go.

SHEILA *(staring at him, agitated)*. When was this?

INSPECTOR *(impressively)*. At the end of January – last year.

SHEILA. What – what did this girl look like?

INSPECTOR. If you'll come over here, I'll show you.

(He moves nearer a light – perhaps standard lamp – and she crosses to him. He produces the photograph. She

5 **influenza:** Grippe.
29 **standard lamp:** Stehlampe.

looks at it closely, recognises it with a little cry, gives a half-stifled sob, and then runs out. The Inspector puts the photograph back into his pocket and stares speculatively after her. The other three stare in amazement for a moment.)

BIRLING. What's the matter with her?

ERIC. She recognised her from the photograph, didn't she?

INSPECTOR. Yes.

BIRLING *(angrily)*. Why the devil do you want to go upsetting the child like that?

INSPECTOR. I didn't do it. She's upsetting herself.

BIRLING. Well – why – why?

INSPECTOR. I don't know – yet. That's something I have to find out.

BIRLING *(still angrily)*. Well – if you don't mind – I'll find out first.

GERALD. Shall I go to her?

BIRLING *(moving)*. No, leave this to me. I must also have a word with my wife – tell her what's happening. *(Turns at door, staring at Inspector angrily.)* We were having a nice little family celebration to-night. And a nasty mess you've made of it now, haven't you?

INSPECTOR *(steadily)*. That's more or less what I was thinking earlier to-night, when I was in the Infirmary looking at what was left of Eva Smith. A nice little promising life there, I thought, and a nasty mess somebody's made of it.

2 **half-stifled:** halb unterdrückt.
3f. **speculatively** (adv.): grüblerisch, nachdenklich.
4 **amazement:** Verwunderung.
10f. **to upset s.o.:** jdn. aus der Fassung bringen.
23 **to make a mess of s.th.:** etwas verpfuschen (*mess:* Durcheinander; Schlamassel; Schweinerei).

(Birling looks as if about to make some retort, then thinks better of it, and goes out, closing door sharply behind him. Gerald and Eric exchange uneasy glances. The Inspector ignores them.)

GERALD. I'd like to have a look at that photograph now, Inspector.

INSPECTOR. All in good time.

GERALD. I don't see why —

INSPECTOR *(cutting in, massively)*. You heard what I said before, Mr. Croft. One line of enquiry at a time. Otherwise we'll all be talking at once and won't know where we are. If you've anything to tell me, you'll have an opportunity of doing it soon.

GERALD *(rather uneasily)*. Well, I don't suppose I have —

ERIC *(suddenly bursting out)*. Look here, I've had enough of this.

INSPECTOR *(dryly)*. I dare say.

ERIC *(uneasily)*. I'm sorry – but you see – we were having a little party – and I've had a few drinks, including rather a lot of champagne – and I've got a headache – and as I'm only in the way here – I think I'd better turn in.

INSPECTOR. And I think you'd better stay here.

ERIC. Why should I?

INSPECTOR. It might be less trouble. If you turn in, you might have to turn out again soon.

GERALD. Getting a bit heavy-handed, aren't you, Inspector?

1 **retort:** scharfe Erwiderung.
17 **I dare say:** allerdings.
21 f. **to turn in** (coll.): ins Bett gehen.
27 **heavy-handed:** streng, unbeugsam.

INSPECTOR. Possibly. But if you're easy with me, I'm easy with you.

GERALD. After all, y'know, we're respectable citizens and not criminals.

INSPECTOR. Sometimes there isn't as much difference as you think. Often, if it was left to me, I wouldn't know where to draw the line.

GERALD. Fortunately, it isn't left to you, is it?

INSPECTOR. No, it isn't. But some things are left to me. Enquiries of this sort, for instance. *(Enter Sheila, who looks as if she's been crying.)* Well, Miss Birling?

SHEILA *(coming in, closing door).* You knew it was me all the time, didn't you?

INSPECTOR. I had an idea it might be – from something the girl herself wrote.

SHEILA. I've told my father – he didn't seem to think it amounted to much – but I felt rotten about it at the time and now I feel a lot worse. Did it make much difference to her?

INSPECTOR. Yes, I'm afraid it did. It was the last real steady job she had. When she lost it – for no reason that she could discover – she decided she might as well try another kind of life.

SHEILA *(miserably).* So I'm really responsible?

INSPECTOR. No, not entirely. A good deal happened to her after that. But you're partly to blame. Just as your father is.

ERIC. But what did Sheila do?

SHEILA *(distressed).* I went to the manager at Milwards and I told him that if they didn't get rid of that girl, I'd

17 **to amount to much:** viel bedeuten (in verneinten Wendungen gebräuchlich).

never go near the place again and I'd persuade mother to close our account with them.

INSPECTOR. And why did you do that?

SHEILA. Because I was in a furious temper.

INSPECTOR. And what had this girl done to make you lose your temper?

SHEILA. When I was looking at myself in the mirror I caught sight of her smiling at the assistant, and I was furious with her. I'd been in a bad temper anyhow.

INSPECTOR. And was it the girl's fault?

SHEILA. No, not really. It was my own fault. *(Suddenly, to Gerald.)* All right, Gerald, you needn't look at me like that. At least, I'm trying to tell the truth. I expect you've done things you're ashamed of too.

GERALD *(surprised)*. Well, I never said I hadn't. I don't see why —

INSPECTOR *(cutting in)*. Never mind about that. You can settle that between you afterwards. *(To Sheila.)* What happened?

SHEILA. I'd gone in to try something on. It was an idea of my own – mother had been against it, and so had the assistant – but I insisted. As soon as I tried it on, I knew they'd been right. It just didn't suit me at all. I looked silly in the thing. Well, this girl had brought the dress up from the workroom, and when the assistant – Miss Francis – had asked her something about it, this girl, to show us what she meant, had held the dress up, as if she was wearing it. And it just suited her. She was the right type for it, just as I was the wrong type. She was a very pretty girl too – with big dark eyes – and that didn't make it any better. Well, when I tried the thing

2 **account:** Konto.

on and looked at myself and knew that it was all wrong, I caught sight of this girl smiling at Miss Francis – as if to say: "Doesn't she look awful" – and I was absolutely furious. I was very rude to both of them, and then I went to the manager and told him that this girl had been very impertinent – and – and — *(She almost breaks down, but just controls herself.)* How could I know what would happen afterwards? If she'd been some miserable plain little creature, I don't suppose I'd have done it. But she was very pretty and looked as if she could take care of herself. I couldn't be sorry for her.

INSPECTOR. In fact, in a kind of way, you might be said to have been jealous of her.

SHEILA. Yes, I suppose so.

INSPECTOR. And so you used the power you had, as a daughter of a good customer and also of a man well-known in the town, to punish the girl just because she made you feel like that?

SHEILA. Yes, but it didn't seem to be anything very terrible at the time. Don't you understand? And if I could help her now, I would —

INSPECTOR *(harshly)*. Yes, but you can't. It's too late. She's dead.

ERIC. My God, it's a bit thick, when you come to think of it —

SHEILA *(stormily)*. Oh shut up, Eric. I know, I know. It's the only time I've ever done anything like that, and I'll never, never do it again to anybody. I've noticed them

6 **impertinent:** unverschämt.
23 **harshly** (adv.): schroff, scharf, rauh.
25 **thick** (coll.): stark, viel.

giving me a sort of look sometimes at Milwards – I noticed it even this afternoon – and I suppose some of them remember. I feel now I can never go there again. Oh – why had this to happen?

INSPECTOR *(sternly)*. That's what I asked myself to-night when I was looking at that dead girl. And then I said to myself: "Well, we'll try to understand why it had to happen." And that's why I'm here, and why I'm not going until I know *all* that happend. Eva Smith lost her job with Birling and Company because the strike failed and they were determined not to have another one. At last she found another job – under what name I don't know – in a big shop, and had to leave there because you were annoyed with yourself and passed the annoyance on to her. Now she had to try something else. So first she changed her name to Daisy Renton —

GERALD *(startled)*. What?

INSPECTOR *(steadily)*. I said she changed her name to Daisy Renton.

GERALD *(pulling himself together)*. D'you mind if I give myself a drink, Sheila?

(Sheila merely nods, still staring at him, and he goes across to the tantalus on the sideboard for a whisky.)

INSPECTOR. Where is your father, Miss Birling?

SHEILA. He went into the drawing-room, to tell my mother what was happening here. Eric, take the Inspector along to the drawing-room. *(As Eric moves, the Inspector looks from Sheila to Gerald, then goes out with Eric.)* Well, Gerald?

5 **sternly** (adv.): streng, unnachgiebig.
24 **tantalus:** verschließbarer Flaschenhalter.
sideboard: Anrichte, Büfett.

GERALD *(trying to smile)*. Well what, Sheila?

SHEILA. How did you come to know this girl – Eva Smith?

GERALD. I didn't.

SHEILA. Daisy Renton then – it's the same thing.

GERALD. Why should I have known her?

SHEILA. Oh don't be stupid. We haven't much time. You gave yourself away as soon as he mentioned her other name.

GERALD. All right. I knew her. Let's leave it at that.

SHEILA. We can't leave it at that.

GERALD *(approaching her)*. Now listen, darling —

SHEILA. No, that's no use. You not only knew her but you knew her very well. Otherwise, you wouldn't look so guilty about it. When did you first get to know her? *(He does not reply.)* Was it after she left Milwards? When she changed her name, as he said, and began to lead a different sort of life? Were you seeing her last spring and summer, during that time when you hardly came near me and said you were so busy? Were you? *(He does not reply but looks at her.)* Yes, of course you were.

GERALD. I'm sorry, Sheila. But it was all over and done with, last summer. I hadn't set eyes on the girl for at least six months. I don't come into this suicide business.

SHEILA. I thought I didn't, half an hour ago.

GERALD. You don't. Neither of us does. So – for God's sake – don't say anything to the Inspector.

SHEILA. About you and this girl?

GERALD. Yes. We can keep it from him.

7 **to give o.s. away:** sich verraten.
27f. **for God's sake:** um Gottes willen.

SHEILA *(laughs rather hysterically)*. Why – you fool – *he knows*. Of course he knows. And I hate to think how much he knows that we don't know yet. You'll see. You'll see.

(She looks at him almost in triumph. He looks crushed. The door slowly opens and the Inspector appears, looking steadily and searchingly at them.)

INSPECTOR. Well?

1 **hysterically** (adv.): hysterisch.
5 **crushed:** (fig.) niedergeschmettert.

Act II

At rise, scene and situation are exactly as they were at end of Act I.

The Inspector remains at the door for a few moments looking at Sheila and Gerald. Then he comes forward, leaving door open behind him.

INSPECTOR *(to Gerald)*. Well?

SHEILA *(with hysterical laugh, to Gerald)*. You see? What did I tell you?

INSPECTOR. What did you tell him?

GERALD *(with an effort)*. Inspector, I think Miss Birling ought to be excused any more of this questioning. She's nothing more to tell you. She's had a long, exciting and tiring day – we were celebrating our engagement, you know – and now she's obviously had about as much as she can stand. You heard her.

SHEILA. He means that I'm getting hysterical now.

INSPECTOR. And are you?

SHEILA. Probably.

INSPECTOR. Well, I don't want to keep you here. I've no more questions to ask you.

SHEILA. No, but you haven't finished asking questions – have you?

INSPECTOR. No.

SHEILA *(to Gerald)*. You see? *(To Inspector.)* Then I'm staying.

GERALD. Why should you? It's bound to be unpleasant and disturbing.

INSPECTOR. And you think young women ought to be protected against unpleasant and disturbing things?

GERALD. If possible – yes.

INSPECTOR. Well, we know one young woman who wasn't, don't we?

GERALD. I suppose I asked for that.

SHEILA. Be careful you don't ask for any more, Gerald.

GERALD. I only meant to say to you — Why stay when you'll hate it?

SHEILA. It can't be any worse for me than it has been. And it might be better.

GERALD *(bitterly)*. I see.

SHEILA. What do you see?

GERALD. You've been through it – and now you want to see somebody else put through it.

SHEILA *(bitterly)*. So that's what you think I'm really like. I'm glad I realised it in time, Gerald.

GERALD. No, no, I didn't mean —

SHEILA *(cutting in)*. Yes, you did. And if you'd really loved me, you couldn't have said that. You listened to that nice story about me. I got that girl sacked from Milwards. And now you've made up your mind I must obviously be a selfish, vindictive creature.

GERALD. I neither said that nor even suggested it.

SHEILA. Then why say I want to see somebody else put through it? That's not what I meant at all.

GERALD. All right then, I'm sorry.

SHEILA. Yes, but you don't believe me. And this is just the wrong time not to believe me.

6 **to ask for s.th.** (coll., fig.): etwas selbst herausfordern; etwas selbst so haben wollen.

23 **vindictive:** rachsüchtig.

INSPECTOR *(massively taking charge).* Allow me, Miss Birling. *(To Gerald.)* I can tell you why Miss Birling wants to stay on and why she says it might be better for her if she did. A girl died to-night. A pretty, lively sort of girl, who never did anybody no harm. But she died in misery and agony – hating life —

SHEILA *(distressed).* Don't please – I know, I know – and I can't stop thinking about it —

INSPECTOR *(ignoring this).* Now Miss Birling has just been made to understand what she did to this girl. She feels responsible. And if she leaves us now, and doesn't hear any more, then she'll feel she's entirely to blame, she'll be alone with her responsibility, the rest of to-night, all to-morrow, all the next night —

SHEILA *(eagerly).* Yes, that's it. And I know I'm to blame – and I'm desperately sorry – but I can't believe – I won't believe – it's simply my fault that in the end she – she committed suicide. That would be too horrible —

INSPECTOR *(sternly to them both).* You see, we have to share something. If there's nothing else, we'll have to share our guilt.

SHEILA *(staring at him).* Yes. That's true. You know. *(She goes closer to him, wonderingly.)* I don't understand about you.

INSPECTOR *(calmly).* There's no reason why you should. *(He regards her calmly while she stares at him wonderingly and dubiously. Now Mrs. Birling enters, briskly*

1 **to take charge:** die Sache in die Hand nehmen, die Leitung übernehmen.

28 **dubiously** (adv.): unschlüssig, im Zweifel.
briskly (adv.): energisch.

and self-confidently, quite out of key with the little scene that has just passed. Sheila feels this at once.)

MRS. BIRLING *(smiling, social).* Good evening, Inspector.

INSPECTOR. Good evening, madam.

MRS. BIRLING *(same easy tone).* I'm Mrs. Birling, y'know. My husband has just explained why you're here, and while we'll be glad to tell you anything you want to know, I don't think we can help you much.

SHEILA. No, Mother – please!

MRS. BIRLING *(affecting great surprise).* What's the matter, Sheila?

SHEILA *(hesitantly).* I know it sounds silly —

MRS. BIRLING. What does?

SHEILA. You see, I feel you're beginning all wrong. And I'm afraid you'll say something or do something that you'll be sorry for afterwards.

MRS. BIRLING. I don't know what you're talking about, Sheila.

SHEILA. We all started like that – so confident, so pleased with ourselves until he began asking us questions.

(Mrs. Birling looks from Sheila to the Inspector.)

MRS. BIRLING. You seem to have made a great impression on this child, Inspector.

INSPECTOR *(coolly).* We often do on the young ones. They're more impressionable.

(He and Mrs. Birling look at each other for a moment. Then Mrs. Birling turns to Sheila again.)

MRS. BIRLING. You're looking tired, dear. I think you

1 **self-confidently** (adv.): selbstsicher.
to be out of key with s.th. (fig.): nicht zu etwas passen.
10 **to affect:** vortäuschen.

ought to go to bed – and forget about this absurd business. You'll feel better in the morning.

SHEILA. Mother, I couldn't possibly go. Nothing could be worse for me. We've settled all that. I'm staying here until I know why that girl killed herself.

MRS. BIRLING. Nothing but morbid curiosity.

SHEILA. No it isn't.

MRS. BIRLING. Please don't contradict me like that. And in any case I don't suppose for a moment that we can understand why the girl committed suicide. Girls of that class —

SHEILA *(urgently, cutting in)*. Mother, don't – please don't. For your own sake, as well as ours, you mustn't —

MRS. BIRLING *(annoyed)*. Mustn't – what? Really, Sheila!

SHEILA *(slowly, carefully now)*. You mustn't try to build up a kind of wall between us and that girl. If you do, then the Inspector will just break it down. And it'll be all the worse when he does.

MRS. BIRLING. I don't understand you. *(To Inspector.)* Do you?

INSPECTOR. Yes. And she's right.

MRS. BIRLING *(haughtily)*. I beg your pardon!

INSPECTOR *(very plainly)*. I said Yes – I do understand her. And she's right.

MRS. BIRLING. That – I consider – is a trifle impertinent, Inspector. *(Sheila gives short hysterical laugh.)* Now, what is it, Sheila?

6 **morbid:** krankhaft.
8 **to contradict s.o.:** jdm. widersprechen.
23 **haughtily** (adv.): arrogant.
26 **a trifle:** ein bißchen, etwas.

SHEILA. I don't know. Perhaps it's because *impertinent* is such a silly word.

MRS. BIRLING. In any case ...

SHEILA. But, Mother, do stop before it's too late.

MRS. BIRLING. If you mean that the Inspector will take offence —

INSPECTOR *(cutting in, calmly)*. No, no, I never take offence.

MRS. BIRLING. I'm glad to hear it. Though I must add that it seems to me that we have more reason for taking offence.

INSPECTOR. Let's leave *offence* out of it, shall we?

GERALD. I think we'd better.

SHEILA. So do I.

MRS. BIRLING *(rebuking them)*. *I'm* talking to the Inspector now, if you don't mind. *(To Inspector, rather grandly.)* I realise that you may have to conduct some sort of enquiry, but I must say that so far you seem to be conducting it in a rather peculiar and offensive manner. You know of course that my husband was Lord Mayor only two years ago and that he's still a magistrate[9] —

GERALD *(cutting in, rather impatiently.)* Mrs. Birling, the Inspector knows all that. And I don't think it's a very good idea to remind him —

SHEILA *(cutting in)*. It's crazy. Stop it, please, Mother.

INSPECTOR *(imperturbable)*. Yes. Now what about Mr. Birling?

MRS. BIRLING. He's coming back in a moment. He's just

5 f. **to take offence:** Anstoß nehmen.
15 **to rebuke:** zurechtweisen, (scharf) tadeln.
27 **imperturbable:** unerschütterlich, gelassen.

talking to my son, Eric, who seems to be in an excitable silly mood.

INSPECTOR. What's the matter with him?

MRS. BIRLING. Eric? Oh – I'm afraid he may have had rather too much to drink to-night. We were having a little celebration here —

INSPECTOR *(cutting in).* Isn't he used to drinking?

MRS. BIRLING. No, of course not. He's only a boy.

INSPECTOR. No, he's a young man. And some young men drink far too much.

SHEILA. And Eric's one of them.

MRS. BIRLING *(very sharply).* Sheila!

SHEILA *(urgently).* I don't want to get poor Eric into trouble. He's probably in enough trouble already. But we really must stop these silly pretences. This isn't the time to pretend that Eric isn't used to drink. He's been steadily drinking too much for the last two years.

MRS. BIRLING *(staggered).* It isn't true. You know him, Gerald – and you're a man – you must know it isn't true.

INSPECTOR *(as Gerald hesitates).* Well, Mr. Croft?

GERALD *(apologetically, to Mrs. Birling).* I'm afraid it is, y'know. Actually I've never seen much of him outside this house – but – well, I have gathered that he does drink pretty hard.

MRS. BIRLING *(bitterly).* And this is the time you choose to tell me.

SHEILA. Yes, of course it is. That's what I meant when I talked about building up a wall that's sure to be knocked flat. It makes it all the harder to bear.

18 **staggered:** schockiert, erschüttert.
22 **apologetically** (adv.): entschuldigend; kleinlaut.

MRS. BIRLING. But it's you – and not the Inspector here – who's doing it —

SHEILA. Yes, but don't you see? *He hasn't started on you yet.*

MRS. BIRLING *(after pause, recovering herself)*. If necessary I shall be glad to answer any questions the Inspector wishes to ask me. Though naturally I don't know anything about this girl.

INSPECTOR *(gravely)*. We'll see, Mrs. Birling.

(Enter Birling, who closes door behind him.)

BIRLING *(rather hot, bothered)*. I've been trying to persuade Eric to go to bed, but he won't. Now he says you told him to stay up. Did you?

INSPECTOR. Yes, I did.

BIRLING. Why?

INSPECTOR. Because I shall want to talk to him, Mr. Birling.

BIRLING. I can't see why you should, but if you must, then I suggest you do it now. Have him in and get it over, then let the lad go.

INSPECTOR. No, I can't do that yet. I'm sorry, but he'll have to wait.

BIRLING. Now look here, Inspector —

INSPECTOR *(cutting in, with authority)*. He must wait his turn.

SHEILA *(to Mrs. Birling)*. You see?

MRS. BIRLING. No, I don't. And please be quiet, Sheila.

BIRLING *(angrily)*. Inspector, I've told you before, I don't like your tone nor the way you're handling this enquiry. And I don't propose to give you much more rope.

11 **bothered:** beunruhigt.
30 f. **to give s.o. rope** (fig.): jdm. Handlungsfreiheit, Spielraum lassen.

INSPECTOR. You needn't give me any rope.

SHEILA *(rather wildly, with laugh)*. No, he's giving us rope – so that we'll hang ourselves.

BIRLING *(to Mrs. Birling)*. What's the matter with that child?

MRS. BIRLING. Over-excited. And she refused to go. *(With sudden anger, to Inspector.)* Well, come along – what is it you want to know?

INSPECTOR *(coolly)*. At the end of January, last year, this girl Eva Smith had to leave Milwards, because Miss Birling compelled them to discharge her, and then she stopped being Eva Smith, looking for a job, and became Daisy Renton, with other ideas. *(Sharply turning on him.)* Mr. Croft, when did you first get to know her?

(An exclamation of surprise from Birling and Mrs. Birling.)

GERALD. Where did you get the idea that I did know her?

SHEILA. It's no use, Gerald. You're wasting time.

INSPECTOR. As soon as I mentioned the name Daisy Renton, it was obvious you'd known her. You gave yourself away at once.

SHEILA *(bitterly)*. Of course he did.

INSPECTOR. And anyhow I knew already. When and where did you first meet her?

GERALD. All right, if you must have it. I met her first, sometime in March last year, in the stalls bar at the Palace. I mean the Palace music hall here in Brumley —

7 **come along** (coll.): dalli! Kommen Sie schon!

27 **stalls bar:** Bar für Sperrsitzkarteninhaber (*stall:* Sperrsitz, Parkettsitz).

28 **music hall:** Varieté(theater).

SHEILA. Well, we didn't think you meant Buckingham Palace[10].

GERALD *(to Sheila)*. Thanks. You're going to be a great help, I can see. You've said your piece, and you're obviously going to hate this, so why on earth don't you leave us to it?

SHEILA. Nothing would induce me. I want to understand exactly what happens when a man says he's so busy at the works that he can hardly ever find time to come and see the girl he's supposed to be in love with. I wouldn't miss it for worlds —

INSPECTOR *(with authority)*. Yes, Mr. Croft – in the stalls bar at the Palace Variety Theatre ...

GERALD. I happened to look in, one night, after a rather long dull day, and as the show wasn't very bright, I went down into the bar for a drink. It's a favourite haunt of women of the town —

MRS. BIRLING. Women of the town?

BIRLING. Yes, yes. But I see no point in mentioning the subject – especially — *(indicating Sheila.)*

MRS. BIRLING. It would be much better if Sheila didn't listen to this story at all.

SHEILA. But you're forgetting I'm supposed to be engaged to the hero of it. Go on, Gerald. You went down into the bar, which is a favourite haunt of women of the town.

GERALD. I'm glad I amuse you —

INSPECTOR *(sharply)*. Come along, Mr. Croft. What happened?

GERALD. I didn't propose to stay long down there. I hate

17 **haunt:** beliebter Aufenthaltsort.
woman of the town: Straßenmädchen.

those hard-eyed dough-faced women. But then I noticed a girl who looked quite different. She was very pretty – soft brown hair and big dark eyes — *(breaks off)* My God!

INSPECTOR. What's the matter?

GERALD *(distressed)*. Sorry – I – well, I've suddenly realised – taken it in properly – that she's dead —

INSPECTOR *(harshly)*. Yes, she's dead.

SHEILA. And probably between us we killed her.

MRS. BIRLING *(sharply)*. Sheila, don't talk nonsense.

SHEILA. You wait, Mother.

INSPECTOR *(to Gerald)*. Go on.

GERALD. She looked young and fresh and charming and altogether out of place down there. And obviously she wasn't enjoying herself. Old Joe Meggarty, half-drunk and goggle-eyed, had wedged her into a corner with that obscene fat carcase of his —

MRS. BIRLING *(cutting in)*. There's no need to be disgusting. And surely you don't mean Alderman Meggarty?

GERALD. Of course I do. He's a notorious womaniser as well as being one of the worst sots and rogues in Brumley —

INSPECTOR. Quite right.

1 **dough-faced:** teiggesichtig, mit blassem Gesicht (*dough:* Teig; [slang] Zaster, Moneten).
7 **to take s.th. in** (fig.): etwas begreifen.
16 **goggle-eyed:** glotzäugig.
to wedge: (hinein)zwängen.
17 **obscene:** widerlich, abscheulich.
carcase: Kadaver.
20 **notorious:** wohlbekannt, berüchtigt.
womaniser (coll.): Schürzenjäger, Casanova.
21 **sot:** Säufer.
rogue: Gauner, Schurke.

MRS. BIRLING *(staggered)*. Well, really! Alderman Meggarty! I must say, we *are* learning something to-night.

SHEILA *(coolly)*. Of course we are. But everybody knows about that horrible old Meggarty. A girl I know had to see him at the Town Hall one afternoon and she only escaped with a torn blouse —

BIRLING *(sharply, shocked)*. Sheila!

INSPECTOR *(to Gerald)*. Go on, please.

GERALD. The girl saw me looking at her and then gave me a glance that was nothing less than a cry for help. So I went across and told Joe Meggarty some nonsense – that the manager had a message for him or something like that – got him out of the way – and then told the girl that if she didn't want any more of that sort of thing, she'd better let me take her out of there. She agreed at once.

INSPECTOR. Where did you go?

GERALD. We went along to the County Hotel, which I knew would be quiet at that time of night, and we had a drink or two and talked.

INSPECTOR. Did she drink much at that time?

GERALD. No. She only had a port and lemonade – or some such concoction. All she wanted was to talk – a little friendliness – and I gathered that Joe Meggarty's advances had left her rather shaken – as well they might —

INSPECTOR. She talked about herself?

GERALD. Yes. I asked her questions about herself. She told me her name was Daisy Renton, that she'd lost both parents, that she came originally from some-

22 **lemonade:** (Zitronen-)Limonade.
23 **concoction** (contempt.): zusammengemixter Trunk.
24 f. **advances:** Annäherungsversuche.

where outside Brumley. She also told me she'd had a job in one of the works here and had had to leave after a strike. She said something about the shop too, but wouldn't say which it was, and she was deliberately vague about what happened. I couldn't get any exact details from her about her past life. She wanted to talk about herself – just because she felt I was interested and friendly – but at the same time she wanted to be Daisy Renton – and not Eva Smith. In fact, I heard that name for the first time to-night. What she did let slip – though she didn't mean to – was that she was desperately hard up and at that moment was actually hungry. I made the people at the County find some food for her.

INSPECTOR. And then you decided to keep her – as your mistress?

MRS. BIRLING. What?

SHEILA. Of course, Mother. It was obvious from the start. Go on, Gerald. Don't mind Mother.

GERALD *(steadily)*. I discovered, not that night but two nights later, when we met again – not accidentally this time of course – that in fact she hadn't a penny and was going to be turned out of the miserable back room she had. It happened that a friend of mine, Charlie Brunswick, had gone off to Canada for six months and had let me have the key of a nice little set of rooms he had – in Morgan Terrace – and had asked me to keep an eye on them for him and use them if I wanted to. So I insisted on Daisy moving into those rooms and I made her take some money to keep her going there. *(Care-*

12 **to be hard up** (coll.): in (Geld-)Schwierigkeiten sein.
30 **to keep s.o. going** (fig.): jdn. am Leben erhalten.

fully, to the Inspector.) I want you to understand that I didn't install her there so that I could make love to her. I made her go to Morgan Terrace because I was sorry for her, and didn't like the idea of her going back to the Palace bar. I didn't ask for anything in return.

INSPECTOR. I see.

SHEILA. Yes, but why are you saying that to him? You ought to be saying it to me.

GERALD. I suppose I ought really. I'm sorry, Sheila. Somehow I —

SHEILA *(cutting in, as he hesitates)*. I know. Somehow he makes you.

INSPECTOR. But she became your mistress?

GERALD. Yes. I suppose it was inevitable. She was young and pretty and warm-hearted – and intensely grateful. I became at once the most important person in her life – you understand?

INSPECTOR. Yes. She was a woman. She was lonely. Were you in love with her?

SHEILA. Just what I was going to ask?

BIRLING *(angrily)*. I really must protest —

INSPECTOR *(turning on him sharply)*. Why should you do any protesting? It was you who turned the girl out in the first place.

BIRLING *(rather taken aback)*. Well, I only did what any employer might have done. And what I was going to say was that I protest against the way in which my daughter, a young unmarried girl, is being dragged into this —

INSPECTOR *(sharply)*. Your daughter isn't living on the moon. She's here in Brumley too.

2 **to install s.o.:** jdn. unterbringen.
25 **taken aback:** verblüfft, überrascht.

SHEILA. Yes, and it was I who had the girl turned out of her job at Milwards. *And* I'm suppposed to be engaged to Gerald. And I'm not a child, don't forget. I've a right to know. *Were* you in love with her, Gerald?

GERALD *(hesitatingly)* It's hard to say. I didn't feel about her as she felt about me.

SHEILA *(with sharp sarcasm)*. Of course not. You were the wonderful Fairy Prince. You must have adored it, Gerald.

GERALD. All right – I did for a time. Nearly any man would have done.

SHEILA. That's probably about the best thing you've said to-night. At least it's honest. Did you go and see her every night?

GERALD. No. I wasn't telling you a complete lie when I said I'd been very busy at the works all that time. We were very busy. But of course I did see a good deal of her.

MRS. BIRLING. I don't think we want any further details of this disgusting affair —

SHEILA *(cutting in)*. I do. And, anyhow, we haven't had any details yet.

GERALD. And you're not going to have any. *(To Mrs. Birling.)* You know, it wasn't disgusting.

MRS. BIRLING. It's disgusting to me.

SHEILA. Yes, but after all, you didn't come into this, did you, Mother?

GERALD. Is there anything else you want to know – that you ought to know?

7 **sarcasm:** Sarkasmus, beißender Spott.
8 **fairy prince:** Märchenprinz.
to adore: hier: ungemein genießen.

INSPECTOR. Yes. When did this affair end?

GERALD. I can tell you exactly. In the first week of September. I had to go away for several weeks then – on business – and by that time Daisy knew it was coming to an end. So I broke it off definitely before I went.

INSPECTOR. How did she take it?

GERALD. Better than I'd hoped. She was – very gallant – about it.

SHEILA *(with irony)*. That was nice for you.

GERALD. No, it wasn't. *(He waits a moment, then in low, troubled tone.)* She told me she'd been happier than she'd ever been before – but that she knew it couldn't last – hadn't expected it to last. She didn't blame me at all. I wish to God she had now. Perhaps I'd feel better about it.

INSPECTOR. She had to move out of those rooms?

GERALD. Yes, we'd agreed about that. She'd saved a little money during the summer – she'd lived very economically on what I'd allowed her – and didn't want to take any more from me, but I insisted on a parting gift of enough money – though it wasn't so very much – to see her through to the end of the year.

INSPECTOR. Did she tell you what she proposed to do after you'd left her?

GERALD. No. She refused to talk about that. I got the idea once or twice from what she said, that she thought of leaving Brumley. Whether she did or not – I don't know. Did she?

INSPECTOR. Yes. She went away for about two months. To some seaside place.

7 **gallant:** tapfer.
19 **to allow:** (eine Geldsumme) geben, zukommen lassen.
21 f. **to see s.o. through:** jdn. durchhalten.

GERALD. By herself?

INSPECTOR. Yes. I think she went away – to be alone, to be quiet, to remember all that had happened between you.

GERALD. How do you know that?

INSPECTOR. She kept a rough sort of diary. And she said there that she had to go away and be quiet and remember "just to make it last longer". She felt there'd never be anything as good again for her – so she had to make it last longer.

GERALD *(gravely)*. I see. Well, I never saw her again, and that's all I can tell you.

INSPECTOR. It's all I want to know from you.

GERALD. In that case – as I'm rather more – upset – by this business than I probably appear to be – and – well, I'd like to be alone for a little while – I'd be glad if you'd let me go.

INSPECTOR. Go where? Home?

GERALD. No. I'll just go out – walk about – for a while, if you don't mind. I'll come back.

INSPECTOR. All right, Mr. Croft.

SHEILA. But just in case you forget – or decide not to come back, Gerald, I think you'd better take this with you. *(She hands him the ring.)*

GERALD. I see. Well, I was expecting this.

SHEILA. I don't dislike you as I did half an hour ago, Gerald. In fact, in some odd way, I rather respect you more than I've ever done before. I knew anyhow you were lying about those months last year when you hardly came near me. I knew there was something fishy about that time. And now at least you've been

31 **fishy** (coll.): hier: faul.

honest. And I believe what you told us about the way you helped her at first. Just out of pity. And it was my fault really that she was so desperate when you first met her. But this has made a difference. You and I aren't the same people who sat down to dinner here. We'd have to start all over again, getting to know each other —

BIRLING. Now, Sheila, I'm not defending him. But you must understand that a lot of young men —

SHEILA. Don't interfere, please, Father. Gerald knows what I mean, and you apparently don't.

GERALD. Yes, I know what you mean. But I'm coming back – if I may.

SHEILA. All right.

MRS. BIRLING. Well, really, I don't know. I think we've just about come to an end of this wretched business —

GERALD. I don't think so. Excuse me.

(He goes out. They watch him go in silence. We hear the front door slam.)

SHEILA *(to Inspector)*. You know, you never showed him that photograph of her.

INSPECTOR. No. It wasn't necessary. And I thought it better not to.

MRS. BIRLING. You have a photograph of this girl?

INSPECTOR. Yes. I think you'd better look at it.

MRS. BIRLING. I don't see any particular reason why I should —

INSPECTOR. Probably not. But you'd better look at it.

MRS. BIRLING. Very well.

(He produces the photograph and she looks hard at it.)

19 **to slam:** zuschlagen, zuknallen.

INSPECTOR *(taking back the photograph)*. You recognise her?

MRS. BIRLING. No. Why should I?

INSPECTOR. Of course she might have changed lately, but I can't believe she could have changed so much.

MRS. BIRLING. I don't understand you, Inspector.

INSPECTOR. You mean you don't choose to do, Mrs. Birling.

MRS. BIRLING *(angrily)*. I meant what I said.

INSPECTOR. You're not telling me the truth.

MRS. BIRLING. I beg your pardon!

BIRLING *(angrily, to Inspector)*. Look here, I'm not going to have this, Inspector. You'll apologise at once.

INSPECTOR. Apologise for what – doing my duty?

BIRLING. No, for being so offensive about it. I'm a public man —

INSPECTOR *(massively)*. Public men, Mr. Birling, have responsibilities as well as privileges.

BIRLING. Possibly. But you weren't asked to come here to talk to me about my responsibilities.

SHEILA. Let's hope not. Though I'm beginning to wonder.

MRS. BIRLING. Does that mean anything, Sheila?

SHEILA. It means that we've no excuse now for putting on airs and that if we've any sense we won't try. Father threw this girl out because she asked for decent wages. I went and pushed her further out, right into the street, just because I was angry and she was pretty. Gerald set her up as his mistress and then dropped her when it

4 **lately** (adv.): unlängst, kürzlich.
7 **to choose to do:** zu tun beschließen.
23 **excuse:** Rechtfertigung; hier auch: Berechtigung.
23 f. **to put on airs:** vornehm tun; sich erhaben fühlen (*air:* Miene, Gebaren).

suited him. And now you're pretending you don't recognise her from that photograph. I admit I don't know why you should, but I know jolly well you did in fact recognise her, from the way you looked. And if you're not telling the truth, why should the Inspector apologise? And can't you see, both of you, you're making it worse?

(She turns away. We hear the front door slam again.)

BIRLING. That was the door again.

MRS. BIRLING. Gerald must have come back.

INSPECTOR. Unless your son has just gone out.

BIRLING. I'll see.

(He goes out quickly. Inspector turns to Mrs. Birling.)

INSPECTOR. Mrs. Birling, you're a member – a prominent member – of the Brumley Women's Charity Organisation,[11] aren't you?

(Mrs. Birling does not reply.)

SHEILA. Go on, Mother. You might as well admit it. *(To Inspector.)* Yes, she is. Why?

INSPECTOR *(calmly)* It's an organisation to which women in distress can appeal for help in various forms. Isn't that so?

MRS. BIRLING *(with dignity)*. Yes. We've done a great deal of useful work in helping deserving cases.

INSPECTOR. There was a meeting of the interviewing committee two weeks ago?

MRS. BIRLING. I dare say there was.

INSPECTOR. You know very well there was, Mrs. Birling. You were in the chair.

15 f. **Women's Charity Organisation:** Frauenhilfsverband; Frauenwohlfahrtsverein.

25 f. **interviewing committee:** hier: Antragsprüfungsausschuß.

29 **to be in the chair** (fig.): den Vorsitz führen.

MRS. BIRLING. And if I was, what business is it of yours?

INSPECTOR *(severely)*. Do you want me to tell you – in plain words?

(Enter Birling, looking rather agitated.)

BIRLING. That must have been Eric.

MRS. BIRLING *(alarmed)*. Have you been up to his room?

BIRLING. Yes. And I called out in both landings. It must have been Eric we heard go out then.

MRS. BIRLING. Silly boy! Where can he have gone to?

BIRLING. I can't imagine. But he was in one of his excitable queer moods, and even though we don't need him here —

INSPECTOR *(cutting in, sharply)*. We do need him here. And if he's not back soon, I shall have to go and find him.

(Birling and Mrs. Birling exchange bewildered and rather frightened glances.)

SHEILA. He's probably just gone to cool off. He'll be back soon.

INSPECTOR *(severely)*. I hope so.

MRS. BIRLING. And why should you hope so?

INSPECTOR. I'll explain why when you've answered my questions, Mrs. Birling.

BIRLING. Is there any reason why my wife should answer questions from you, Inspector?

INSPECTOR. Yes, a very good reason. You'll remember that Mr. Croft told us – quite truthfully, I believe – that he hadn't spoken to or seen Eva Smith since last September. But Mrs. Birling spoke to and saw her only two weeks ago.

SHEILA *(astonished)*. Mother!

7 **landing:** Treppenabsatz.

BIRLING. Is this true?

MRS. BIRLING *(after a pause)*. Yes, quite true.

INSPECTOR. She appealed to your organisation for help?

MRS. BIRLING. Yes.

INSPECTOR. Not as Eva Smith?

MRS. BIRLING. No. Nor as Daisy Renton.

INSPECTOR. As what then?

MRS. BIRLING. First, she called herself Mrs. Birling –

BIRLING *(astounded)*. *Mrs. Birling!*

MRS. BIRLING. Yes. I think it was simply a piece of gross impertinence – quite deliberate – and naturally that was one of the things that prejudiced me against her case.

BIRLING. And I should think so! Damned impudence!

INSPECTOR. You admit being prejudiced against her case?

MRS. BIRLING. Yes.

SHEILA. Mother, she's just died a horrible death – don't forget.

MRS. BIRLING. I'm very sorry. But I think she had only herself to blame.

INSPECTOR. Was it owing to your influence, as the most prominent member of the committee, that help was refused the girl?

MRS. BIRLING. Possibly.

INSPECTOR. Was it or was it not your influence?

MRS. BIRLING *(stung)*. Yes, it was. I didn't like her manner. She'd impertinently made use of our name, though she pretended afterwards it just happened to

9 **astounded:** äußerst überrascht, sehr erstaunt.
10 **gross:** ungeheuerlich.
11 **impertinence:** Unverschämtheit.
14 **impudence:** Unverschämtheit.
26 **stung:** (schmerzhaft) getroffen (Part. Perf. von *to sting*).

be the first she thought of. She had to admit, after I began questioning her, that she had no claim to the name, that she wasn't married, and that the story she told at first – about a husband who'd deserted her – was quite false. It didn't take me long to get the truth – or some of the truth – out of her.

INSPECTOR. Why did she want help?

MRS. BIRLING. You know very well why she wanted help.

INSPECTOR. No, I don't. I know why she *needed* help. But as I wasn't there, I don't know what she asked from your committee.

MRS. BIRLING. I don't think we need discuss it.

INSPECTOR. You have no hope of *not* discussing it, Mrs. Birling.

MRS. BIRLING. If you think you can bring any pressure to bear upon me, Inspector, you're quite mistaken. Unlike the other three, I did nothing I'm ashamed of or that won't bear investigation. The girl asked for assistance. We are asked to look carefully into the claims made upon us. I wasn't satisfied with this girl's claim – she seemed to me to be not a good case – and so I used my influence to have it refused. And in spite of what's happened to the girl since, I consider I did my duty. So if I prefer not to discuss it any further, you have no power to make me change my mind.

INSPECTOR. Yes I have.

MRS. BIRLING. No you haven't. Simply because I've done nothing wrong – and you know it.

INSPECTOR *(very deliberately)*. I think you did something terribly wrong – and that you're going to spend the rest

15 f. **to bring pressure to bear upon s. o.:** auf jdn. Druck ausüben.
18 **to bear investigation:** einer Untersuchung standhalten.

of your life regretting it. I wish you'd been with me to-night in the Infirmary. You'd have seen —

SHEILA *(bursting in)*. No, no, please! Not that again. I've imagined it enough already.

INSPECTOR *(very deliberately)*. Then the next time you imagine it, just remember that this girl was going to have a child.

SHEILA *(horrified)*. No! Oh – horrible – horrible! How could she have wanted to kill herself?

INSPECTOR. Because she'd been turned out and turned down too many times. This was the end.

SHEILA. Mother, you must have known.

INSPECTOR. It was because she was going to have a child that she went for assistance to your mother's committee.

BIRLING. Look here, this wasn't Gerald Croft —

INSPECTOR *(cutting in, sharply)*. No, no. Nothing to do with him.

SHEILA. Thank goodness for that! Though I don't know why I should care now.

INSPECTOR *(to Mrs. Birling)*. And you've nothing further to tell me, eh?

MRS. BIRLING. I'll tell you what I told her. Go and look for the father of the child. It's his responsibility.

INSPECTOR. That doesn't make it any the less yours. She came to you for help, at a time when no woman could have needed it more. And you not only refused it yourself but saw to it that the others refused it too. She was here alone, friendless, almost penniless, desperate. She needed not only money, but advice, sympathy,

19 **thank goodness:** Gott sei Dank!
28 **to see to it that:** dafür sorgen, daß.

friendliness. You've had children. You must have known what she was feeling. And you slammed the door in her face.

SHEILA *(with feeling)*. Mother, I think it was cruel and vile.

BIRLING *(dubiously)*. I must say, Sybil, that when this comes out at the inquest, it isn't going to do us much good. The Press might easily take it up —

MRS. BIRLING *(agitated now)*. Oh, stop it, both of you. And please remember before you start accusing me of anything again that it wasn't I who had her turned out of her employment – which probably began it all. *(Turning to Inspector.)* In the circumstances I think I was justified. The girl had begun by telling us a pack of lies. Afterwards, when I got at the truth, I discovered that she knew who the father was, she was quite certain about that, and so I told her it was her business to make him responsible. If he refused to marry her – and in my opinion he ought to be compelled to – then he must at least support her.

INSPECTOR. And what did she reply to that?

MRS. BIRLING. Oh – a lot of silly nonsense!

INSPECTOR. What was it?

MRS. BIRLING. Whatever it was, I know it made me finally lose all patience with her. She was giving herself ridiculous airs. She was claiming elaborate fine feelings and scruples that were simply absurd in a girl in her position.

5 **vile:** gemein.

7 **inquest** (jur.): gerichtliche Untersuchung der Todesursache bei nicht natürlichen Todesfällen.

25 f. **to give o.s. airs:** vornehm tun.

27 **scruples** (pl.): Bedenken.

INSPECTOR *(very sternly)*. Her position now is that she lies with a burnt-out inside on a slab. *(As Birling tries to protest, turns on him.)* Don't stammer and yammer at me again, man. I'm losing all patience with you people. *What did she say?*

MRS. BIRLING *(rather cowed)*. She said that the father was only a youngster – silly and wild and drinking too much. There couldn't be any question of marrying him – it would be wrong for them both. He had given her money but she didn't want to take any more money from him.

INSPECTOR. Why didn't she want to take any more money from him?

MRS. BIRLING. All a lot of nonsense – I didn't believe a word of it.

INSPECTOR. I'm not asking you if you believed it. I want to know what she said. Why didn't she want to take any more money from this boy?

MRS. BIRLING. Oh – she had some fancy reason. As if a girl of that sort would ever refuse money!

INSPECTOR *(sternly)*. I warn you, you're making it worse for yourself. What reason did she give for not taking any more money?

MRS. BIRLING. Her story was – that he'd said something one night, when he was drunk, that gave her the idea that it wasn't his money.

INSPECTOR. Where had he got it from then?

MRS. BIRLING. He'd stolen it.

2 **slab:** (Holz-)Platte, Brett (vgl. *on the slab* [coll.]: im Leichenschauhaus).

3 **to stammer:** stammeln.
to yammer: jammern.

6 **cowed:** eingeschüchtert, geduckt.

INSPECTOR. So she'd come to you for assistance because she didn't want to take stolen money?

MRS. BIRLING. That's the story she finally told, after I'd refused to believe her original story – that she was a married woman who'd been deserted by her husband. I didn't see any reason to believe that one story should be any truer than the other. Therefore, you're quite wrong to suppose I shall regret what I did.

INSPECTOR. But if her story was true, if this boy had been giving her stolen money, then she came to you for help because she wanted to keep this youngster out of any more trouble – isn't that so?

MRS. BIRLING. Possibly. But it sounded ridiculous to me. So I was perfectly justified in advising my committee not to allow her claim for assistance.

INSPECTOR. You're not even sorry now, when you know what happened to the girl?

MRS. BIRLING. I'm sorry she should have come to such a horrible end. But I accept no blame for it at all.

INSPECTOR. Who is to blame then?

MRS. BIRLING. First, the girl herself.

SHEILA *(bitterly)*. For letting Father and me have her chucked out of her jobs!

MRS. BIRLING. Secondly, I blame the young man who was the father of the child she was going to have. If, as she said, he didn't belong to her class, and was some drunken young idler, then that's all the more reason why he shouldn't escape. He should be made an example of. If the girl's death is due to anybody, then it's due to him.

23 **to chuck s.o. out** (coll.): jdn. rausschmeißen, entlassen.
27 **idler:** Müßiggänger.
28 **to make an example of s.o.:** an jdm. ein Exempel statuieren.

INSPECTOR. And if her story is true – that he was stealing money —

MRS. BIRLING *(rather agitated now)*. There's no point in assuming that —

INSPECTOR. But suppose we do, what then?

MRS. BIRLING. Then he'd be entirely responsible – because the girl wouldn't have come to us, and have been refused assistance, if it hadn't been for him —

INSPECTOR. So he's the chief culprit anyhow.

MRS. BIRLING. Certainly. And he ought to be dealt with very severely —

SHEILA *(with sudden alarm)*. Mother – stop – stop!

BIRLING. Be quiet, Sheila!

SHEILA. But don't you see —

MRS. BIRLING *(severely)*. You're behaving like an hysterical child to-night. *(Sheila begins crying quietly. Mrs. Birling turns to Inspector.)* And if you'd take some steps to find this young man and then make sure that he's compelled to confess in public his responsibility – instead of staying here asking quite unnecessary questions – then you really would be doing your duty.

INSPECTOR *(grimly)*. Don't worry, Mrs. Birling. I shall do my duty. *(He looks at his watch.)*

MRS. BIRLING *(triumphantly)*. I'm glad to hear it.

INSPECTOR. No hushing up, eh? Make an example of the young man, eh? Public confession of responsibility – um?

9 **culprit:** Schuldiger, Missetäter.

17 f. **to take steps:** Schritte unternehmen.
to make sure that: sich davon überzeugen, daß; hier auch: dafür Sorge tragen, daß.

25 **to hush up:** vertuschen.

MRS. BIRLING. Certainly. I consider it your duty. And now no doubt you'd like to say good night.

INSPECTOR. Not yet. I'm waiting.

MRS. BIRLING. Waiting for what?

INSPECTOR. To do my duty.

SHEILA *(distressed)*. Now, Mother – don't you see?

MRS. BIRLING *(understanding now)*. But surely ... I mean ... it's ridiculous ...

(She stops, and exchanges a frightened glance with her husband.)

BIRLING *(terrified now)*. Look, Inspector, you're not trying to tell us that – that my boy – is mixed up in this —?

INSPECTOR *(sternly)*. If he is, then we know what to do, don't we? Mrs. Birling has just told us.

BIRLING *(thunderstruck)*. My God! But – look here —

MRS. BIRLING *(agitated)*. I don't believe it. I *won't* believe it ...

SHEILA. Mother – I begged you and begged you to stop —

(Inspector holds up a hand. We hear the front door. They wait, looking towards door. Eric enters, looking extremely pale and distressed. He meets their enquiring stares.

Curtain falls quickly.)

16 **thunderstruck:** wie vom Donner gerührt.

Act III

Exactly as at end of Act II. Eric is standing just inside the room and the others are staring at him.

ERIC. You know, don't you?

INSPECTOR *(as before)*. Yes, we know.

(Eric shuts the door and comes further in.)

MRS. BIRLING *(distressed)*. Eric, I can't believe it. There must be some mistake. You don't know what we've been saying.

SHEILA. It's a good job for him he doesn't, isn't it?

ERIC. Why?

SHEILA. Because Mother's been busy blaming everything on the young man who got this girl into trouble, and saying he shouldn't escape and should be made an example of —

BIRLING. That's enough, Sheila.

ERIC *(bitterly)*. You haven't made it any easier for me, have you, Mother?

MRS. BIRLING. But I didn't know it was *you* – I never dreamt. Besides, you're not that type – you don't get drunk —

SHEILA. Of course he does. I told you he did.

ERIC. *You* told her. Why, you little sneak!

SHEILA. No, that's not fair, Eric. I could have told her months ago, but of course I didn't. I only told her to-

23 **sneak** (coll.): Petze(r).

night because I knew everything was coming out – it was simply bound to come out to-night – so I thought she might as well know in advance. Don't forget – I've already been through it.

MRS. BIRLING. Sheila, I simply don't understand your attitude.

BIRLING. Neither do I. If you'd had any sense of loyalty —

INSPECTOR *(cutting in, smoothly)*. Just a minute, Mrs. Birling. There'll be plenty of time, when I've gone, for you all to adjust your family relationships. But now I must hear what your son has to tell me. *(Sternly, to the three of them.)* And I'll be obliged if you'll let us get on without any further interruptions. *(Turning to Eric.)* Now then.

ERIC *(miserably)*. Could I have a drink first?

BIRLING *(explosively)*. No.

INSPECTOR *(firmly)*. Yes. *(As Birling looks like interrupting explosively.)* I know – he's your son and this is your house – but look at him. He needs a drink now just to see him through.

BIRLING *(to Eric)*. All right. Go on.

(Eric goes for a whisky. His whole manner of handling the decanter and then the drink shows his familiarity with quick heavy drinking. The others watch him narrowly.)

(Bitterly.) I understand a lot of things now I didn't understand before.

INSPECTOR. Don't start on that. I want to get on. *(To Eric.)* When did you first meet this girl?

ERIC. One night last November.

10 **to adjust:** in Ordnung bringen, regeln.

12 **to be obliged:** zu Dank verpflichtet sein.

INSPECTOR. Where did you meet her?

ERIC. In the Palace bar. I'd been there an hour or so with two or three chaps. I was a bit squiffy.

INSPECTOR. What happened then?

ERIC. I began talking to her, and stood her a few drinks. I was rather far gone by the time we had to go.

INSPECTOR. Was she drunk too?

ERIC. She told me afterwards that she was a bit, chiefly because she'd not had much to eat that day.

INSPECTOR. Why had she gone there —?

ERIC. She wasn't the usual sort. But – well, I suppose she didn't know what to do. There was some woman who wanted her to go there. I never quite understood about that.

INSPECTOR. You went with her to her lodgings that night?

ERIC. Yes, I insisted – it seems. I'm not very clear about it, but afterwards she told me she didn't want me to go in but that – well, I was in that state when a chap easily turns nasty – and I threatened to make a row.

INSPECTOR. So she let you in?

ERIC. And that's when it happened. And I didn't even remember – that's the hellish thing. Oh – my God! – how stupid it all is!

MRS. BIRLING *(with a cry)*. Oh – Eric – how could you?

BIRLING *(sharply)*. Sheila, take your mother along to the drawing-room —

SHEILA *(protesting)*. But – I want to —

BIRLING *(very sharply)*. You heard what I said. *(Gentler.)* Go on, Sybil.

5 **to stand s.o. a drink** (coll.): jdm. einen ausgeben, ein Getränk spendieren.

6 **far gone:** hier: schwer betrunken, total ‚weggetreten'.

19 **row:** Krawall, Radau.

(He goes to open the door while Sheila takes her mother out. Then he closes it and comes in.)

INSPECTOR. When did you meet her again?

ERIC. About a fortnight afterwards.

INSPECTOR. By appointment?

ERIC. No. And I couldn't remember her name or where she lived. It was all very vague. But I happened to see her again in the Palace bar.

INSPECTOR. More drinks?

ERIC. Yes, though that time I wasn't so bad.

INSPECTOR. But you took her home again?

ERIC. Yes. And this time we talked a bit. She told me something about herself and I talked too. Told her my name and what I did.

INSPECTOR. And you made love again?

ERIC. Yes. I wasn't in love with her or anything – but I liked her – she was pretty and a good sport —

BIRLING *(harshly)*. So you had to go to bed with her?

ERIC. Well, I'm old enough to be married, aren't I, and I'm not married, and I hate these fat old tarts round the town – the ones I see some of your respectable friends with —

BIRLING *(angrily)*. I don't want any of that talk from you —

INSPECTOR *(very sharply)*. I don't want any of it from either of you. Settle it afterwards. *(To Eric.)* Did you arrange to see each other after that?

ERIC. Yes. And the next time – or the time after that – she

4 **fortnight:** vierzehn Tage.
5 **appointment:** Verabredung.
17 **to be a good sport** (coll.): kein Spielverderber sein.
20 **tart** (slang): Flittchen.

told me she thought she was going to have a baby. She wasn't quite sure. And then she was.

INSPECTOR. And of course she was very worried about it?

ERIC. Yes, and so was I. I was in a hell of a state about it.

INSPECTOR. Did she suggest that you ought to marry her?

ERIC. No. She didn't want me to marry her. Said I didn't love her – and all that. In a way, she treated me – as if I were a kid. Though I was nearly as old as she was.

INSPECTOR. So what did you propose to do?

ERIC. Well, she hadn't a job – and didn't feel like trying again for one – and she'd no money left – so I insisted on giving her enough money to keep her going – until she refused to take any more —

INSPECTOR. How much did you give her altogether?

ERIC. I suppose – about fifty pounds all told.

BIRLING. Fifty pounds – on top of drinking and going round the town! Where did you get fifty pounds from? *(As Eric does not reply.)*

INSPECTOR. That's my question too.

ERIC *(miserably)*. I got it – from the office —

BIRLING. *My* office?

ERIC. Yes.

INSPECTOR. You mean – you stole the money?

ERIC. Not really.

BIRLING *(angrily)*. What do you mean – *not really?* *(Eric does not reply because now Mrs. Birling and Sheila come back.)*

SHEILA. This isn't my fault.

MRS. BIRLING *(to Birling)*. I'm sorry, Arthur, but I simply

8 **kid** (coll.): (kleines) Kind.
15 **all told:** hier: insgesamt.
16 **on top of:** obendrein, noch dazu.

couldn't stay in there. I had to know what's happening.

BIRLING *(savagely)*. Well, I can tell you what's happening. He's admitted he was responsible for the girl's condition, and now he's telling us he supplied her with money he stole from the office.

MRS. BIRLING *(shocked)*. Eric! You stole money?

ERIC. No, not really. I intended to pay it back.

BIRLING. We've heard that story before. How could you have paid it back?

ERIC. I'd have managed somehow. I had to have some money —

BIRLING. I don't understand how you could take as much as that out of the office without somebody knowing.

ERIC. There were some small accounts to collect, and I asked for cash —

BIRLING. Gave the firm's receipt and then kept the money, eh?

ERIC. Yes.

BIRLING. You must give me a list of those accounts. I've got to cover this up as soon as I can. You damned fool – why didn't you come to me when you found yourself in this mess?

ERIC. Because you're not the kind of father a chap could go to when he's in trouble – that's why.

BIRLING *(angrily)*. Don't talk to me like that. Your trouble is – you've been spoilt —

INSPECTOR *(cutting in)*. And my trouble is – that I haven't much time. You'll be able to divide the responsibility

3 **savagely** (adv.): wütend, wild.
17 **receipt:** Quittung.
21 **to cover s.th. up:** (fig.): etwas verdecken, vertuschen.

between you when I've gone. *(To Eric.)* Just one last question, that's all. The girl discovered that this money you were giving her was stolen, didn't she?

ERIC *(miserably).* Yes. That was the worst of all. She wouldn't take any more, and she didn't want to see me again. *(Sudden startled tone.)* Here, but how did you know that? Did she tell you?

INSPECTOR. No. She told me nothing. I never spoke to her.

SHEILA. She told Mother.

MRS. BIRLING *(alarmed).* Sheila!

SHEILA. Well, he has to know.

ERIC *(to Mrs. Birling).* She told you? Did she come here – but then she couldn't have done, she didn't even know I lived here. What happened? *(Mrs. Birling, distressed, shakes her head but does not reply.)* Come on, don't just look like that. Tell me – tell me – what happened?

INSPECTOR *(with calm authority).* I'll tell you. She went to your mother's committee for help, after she'd done with you. Your mother refused that help.

ERIC *(nearly at breaking point).* Then – you killed her. She came to you to protect me – and you turned her away – yes, and you killed her – and the child she'd have had too – my child – your own grandchild – you killed them both – damn you, damn you —

MRS. BIRLING *(very distressed now).* No – Eric – please – I didn't know – I didn't understand —

ERIC *(almost threatening her).* You don't understand anything. You never did. You never even tried – you —

SHEILA *(frightened).* Eric, don't – don't —

14 **to have done** (coll.): hier: Schluß machen.

BIRLING *(furious, intervening).* Why, you hysterical young fool – get back – or I'll —

INSPECTOR *(taking charge, masterfully). Stop! (They are suddenly quiet, staring at him.)* And be quiet for a moment and listen to me. I don't need to know any more. Neither do you. This girl killed herself – and died a horrible death. But each of you helped to kill her. Remember that. Never forget it. *(He looks from one to the other of them carefully.)* But then I don't think you ever will. Remember what you did, Mrs. Birling. You turned her away when she most needed help. You refused her even the pitiable little bit of organised charity you had in your power to grant her. Remember what you did —

ERIC *(unhappily).* My God – I'm not likely to forget.

INSPECTOR. Just used her for the end of a stupid drunken evening, as if she was an animal, a thing, not a person. No, you won't forget. *(He looks at Sheila.)*

SHEILA *(bitterly).* I know. I had her turned out of a job. I started it.

INSPECTOR. You helped – but didn't start it. *(Rather savagely, to Birling.)* You started it. She wanted twenty-five shillings a week instead of twenty-two and sixpence. You made her pay a heavy price for that. And now she'll make you pay a heavier price still.

BIRLING *(unhappily).* Look, Inspector – I'd give thousands – yes, thousands —

INSPECTOR. You're offering the money at the wrong time, Mr. Birling. *(He makes a move as if concluding the session, possibly shutting up notebook, etc. Then*

1 **to intervene:** sich einmischen.
12 **pitiable:** armselig, jämmerlich.

surveys them sardonically.) No, I don't think any of you will forget. Nor that young man, Croft, though he at least had some affection for her and made her happy for a time. Well, Eva Smith's gone. You can't do her any more harm. And you can't do her any good now, either. You can't even say "I'm sorry, Eva Smith."

SHEILA *(who is crying quietly)*. That's the worst of it.

INSPECTOR. But just remember this. One Eva Smith has gone – but there are millions and millions and millions of Eva Smiths and John Smiths still left with us, with their lives, their hopes and fears, their suffering, and chance of happiness, all intertwined with our lives, with what we think and say and do. We don't live alone. We are members of one body. We are responsible for each other. And I tell you that the time will soon come when, if men will not learn that lesson, then they will be taught it in fire and blood and anguish. Good night.

(He walks straight out, leaving them staring, subdued and wondering. Sheila is still quietly crying. Mrs. Birling has collapsed into a chair. Eric is brooding desperately. Birling, the only active one, hears the front door slam, moves hesitatingly towards the door, stops, looks gloomily at the other three, then pours himself out a drink, which he hastily swallows.)

1 **to survey:** mustern.
sardonically (adv.): boshaft, hämisch.
3 **affection:** Zuneigung.
13 **to intertwine:** verflechten.
18 **anguish:** Schmerz, Qual.
20 **to subdue:** überwältigen, bezwingen.
22 **to collapse:** zusammenbrechen, zusammenklappen.
to brood: brüten.

BIRLING *(angrily to Eric).* You're the one I blame for this.

ERIC. I'll bet I am.

BIRLING *(angrily).* Yes, and you don't realise yet all you've done. Most of this is bound to come out. There'll be a public scandal.

ERIC. Well, I don't care now.

BIRLING. You! You don't seem to care about anything. But I care. I was almost certain for a knighthood in the next Honours List —

(Eric laughs rather hysterically, pointing at him.)

ERIC *(laughing).* Oh – for God's sake! What does it matter now whether they give you a knighthood or not?

BIRLING *(stormily).* It doesn't matter to you. Apparently nothing matters to you. But it may interest you to know that until every penny of that money you stole is repaid, you'll work for nothing. And there's going to be no more of this drinking round the town – and picking up women in the Palace bar —

MRS. BIRLING *(coming to life).* I should think not. Eric, I'm absolutely ashamed of you.

ERIC. Well, I don't blame you. But don't forget I'm ashamed of you as well – yes, both of you.

BIRLING *(angrily).* Drop that. There's every excuse for what both your mother and I did – it turned out unfortunately, that's all —

SHEILA *(scornfully). That's all.*

BIRLING. Well, what have you to say?

SHEILA. I don't know where to begin.

BIRLING. Then don't begin. Nobody wants you to.

2 **I'll bet** (coll.): aber sicher, und ob (von *to bet* ›wetten‹).
23 **drop that:** laß dies, hör damit auf!
26 **scornfully** (adv.): verächtlich.

SHEILA. I behaved badly too. I know I did. I'm ashamed of it. But now you're beginning all over again to pretend that nothing much has happened —

BIRLING. Nothing much has happened! Haven't I already said there'll be a public scandal – unless we're lucky – and who here will suffer from that more than I will?

SHEILA. But that's not what I'm talking about. I don't care about that. The point is, you don't seem to have learnt anything.

BIRLING. Don't I? Well, you're quite wrong there. I've learnt plenty to-night. And you don't want me to tell you what I've learnt, I hope. When I look back on to-night – when I think of what I was feeling when the five of us sat down to dinner at that tabel —

ERIC *(cutting in)*. Yes, and do you remember what you said to Gerald and me after dinner, when you were feeling so pleased with yourself? You told us that a man has to make his own way, look afer himself and mind his own business, and that we weren't to take any notice of these cranks who tell us that everybody has to look after everybody else, as if we were all mixed up together. Do you remember? Yes – and then one of those cranks walked in – the Inspector. *(Laughs bitterly.)* I didn't notice you told him that it's every man for himself.

SHEILA *(sharply attentive)*. Is that when the Inspector came, just after Father had said that?

ERIC. Yes. What of it?

MRS. BIRLING. Now what's the matter, Sheila.

SHEILA *(slowly)*. It's queer – very queer – *(she looks at them reflectively.)*

28 **what of it?:** na und?
31 **reflectively** (adv.): nachdenklich.

MRS. BIRLING *(with some excitement)*. I know what you're going to say. Because I've been wondering myself.

SHEILA. It doesn't much matter now, of course – but *was* he really a police inspector?

BIRLING. Well, if he wasn't, it matters a devil of a lot. Makes all the difference.

SHEILA. No, it doesn't.

BIRLING. Dont't talk rubbish. Of course it does.

SHEILA. Well, it doesn't to me. And it oughtn't to you, either.

MRS. BIRLING. Don't be childish, Sheila.

SHEILA *(flaring up)*. I'm not being. If you want to know, it's you two who are being childish – trying not to face the facts.

BIRLING. I won't have that sort of talk. Any more of that and you leave this room.

ERIC. That'll be terrible for her, won't it?

SHEILA. I'm going anyhow in a minute or two. But don't you see, if all that's come out to-night is true, then it doesn't much matter who it was who made us confess. And it *was* true, wasn't it? You turned the girl out of one job, and I had her turned out of another. Gerald kept her – at a time when he was supposed to be too busy to see me. Eric – well, we know what Eric did. And Mother hardened her heart and gave her the final push that finished her. That's what's important – and not whether a man is a police inspector or not.

ERIC. He was our police inspector all right.

SHEILA. That's what I mean, Eric. But if it's any comfort to you – and it isn't to me – I have an idea – and I had it

5 **a devil of a lot** (coll.): verdammt viel.
12 **to flare up** (fig.): aufbrausen.

all along vaguely – that there was something curious about him. He never seemed like an ordinary police inspector —

BIRLING *(rather excited).* You're right. I felt it too. *(To Mrs. Birling.)* Didn't you?

MRS. BIRLING. Well, I must say his manner was quite extraordinary; so – so rude – and assertive —

BIRLING. Then look at the way he talked to me. Telling me to shut up – and so on. He must have known I was an ex-Lord Mayor and a magistrate and so forth. Besides – the way he talked – you remember. I mean, they don't *talk* like that. I've had dealings with dozens of them.

SHEILA. All right. But it doesn't make any real difference, y'know.

MRS. BIRLING. Of course it does.

ERIC. No, Sheila's right. It doesn't.

BIRLING *(angrily).* That's comic, that is, coming from you. You're the one it makes *most* difference to. You've confessed to theft, and now he knows all about it, and he can bring it out at the inquest, and then if necessary carry it to court. He can't do anything to your mother and Sheila and me – except perhaps make us look a bit ashamed of ourselves in public – but as for you, he can ruin you. You know.

SHEILA *(slowly).* We hardly ever told him anything he didn't know. Did you notice that?

BIRLING. That's nothing. He had a bit of information, left by the girl, and made a few smart guesses – but the fact remains that if we hadn't talked so much, he'd have

20 **theft:** Diebstahl.
29 **smart:** gescheit, klug.

had little to go on. *(Looks angrily at them.)* And really, when I come to think of it, why you all had to go letting everything come out like that, beats me.

SHEILA. It's all right talking like that now. But he made us confess.

MRS. BIRLING. He certainly didn't make me *confess* – as you call it. I told him quite plainly that I thought I had done no more than my duty.

SHEILA. Oh – Mother!

BIRLING. The fact is, you allowed yourselves to be bluffed. Yes – bluffed.

MRS. BIRLING *(protesting)*. Now really – Arthur.

BIRLING. No, not you, my dear. But these two. That fellow obviously didn't like us. He was prejudiced from the start. Probably a Socialist or some sort of crank – he talked like one. And then, instead of standing up to him, you let him bluff you into talking about your private affairs. You ought to have stood up to him.

ERIC *(sulkily)*. Well, I didn't notice you standing up to him.

BIRLING. No, because by that time you'd admitted you'd been taking money. What chance had I after that? I was a fool not to have insisted upon seeing him alone.

ERIC. That wouldn't have worked.

SHEILA. Of course it wouldn't.

MRS. BIRLING. Really, from the way you children talk, you might be wanting to help him instead of us. Now just be quiet so that your father can decide what we ought to do. *(Looks expectantly at Birling.)*

3 **to beat s.o.** (fig.): jdn. verblüffen; auch: ‚fertigmachen'.
10f. **to be bluffed:** geblufft, getäuscht werden.
16f. **to stand up to s.o.:** jdm. die Stirn bieten.

BIRLING *(dubiously)*. Yes – well. We'll have to do something – and get to work quickly too. *(As he hesitates there is a ring at the front door. They look at each other in alarm.)* Now who's this? Had I better go?

MRS. BIRLING. No. Edna'll go. I asked her to wait up to make us some tea.

SHEILA. It might be Gerald coming back.

BIRLING *(relieved)*. Yes, of course. I'd forgotten about him.

(Edna appears.)

EDNA. It's Mr. Croft.

(Gerald appears, and Edna withdraws.)

GERALD. I hope you don't mind my coming back?

MRS. BIRLING. No, of course not, Gerald.

GERALD. I had a special reason for coming. When did that Inspector go?

SHEILA. Only a few minutes ago. He put us all through it —

MRS. BIRLING *(warningly)*. Sheila!

SHEILA. Gerald might as well know.

BIRLING *(hastily)*. Now – now – we needn't bother him with all that stuff.

SHEILA. All right. *(To Gerald.)* But we're all in it – up to the neck. It got worse after you left.

GERALD. How did he behave?

SHEILA. He was – frightening.

BIRLING. If you ask me, he behaved in a very peculiar and suspicious manner.

MRS. BIRLING. The rude way he spoke to Mr. Birling and me – it was quite extraordinary!

5 **to wait up:** hier: aufbleiben.
21 **to bother:** belästigen.
28 **suspicious:** verdächtig.

GERALD. Hm – hm!

(They all look enquiringly at Gerald.)

BIRLING *(excitedly)*. You know something. What is it?

GERALD *(slowly)*. That man wasn't a police officer.

BIRLING *(astounded)*. What?

MRS. BIRLING. Are you certain?

GERALD. I'm almost certain. That's what I came back to tell you.

BIRLING *(excitedly)*. Good lad! You asked about him, eh?

GERALD. Yes. I met a police sergeant I know down the road. I asked him about this Inspector Goole and described the chap carefully to him. He swore there wasn't any Inspector Goole or anybody like him on the force here.

BIRLING. You didn't tell him —

GERALD *(cutting in)*. No, no. I passed it off by saying I'd been having an argument with somebody. But the point is – this sergeant was dead certain they hadn't any inspector at all like the chap who came here.

BIRLING *(excitedly)*. By Jingo! A fake!

MRS. BIRLING *(triumphantly)*. Didn't I tell you? Didn't I say I couldn't imagine a real police inspector talking like that to us?

GERALD. Well, you were right. There isn't any such inspector. We've been had.

10 **police sergeant:** Polizeiwachtmeister.
13 f. **on the force:** bei der Polizei.
16 **to pass s.th. off:** hier: von etwas ablenken.
17 **argument:** Auseinandersetzung, Streit.
18 **dead** (adv.): völlig, absolut.
20 **by Jingo:** Donnerwetter!
fake: Schwindler, Betrüger.
25 **to have s.o.** (coll.): jdn. reinlegen.

BIRLING *(beginning to move)*. I'm going to make certain of this.

MRS. BIRLING. What are you going to do?

BIRLING. Ring up the Chief Constable – Colonel Roberts.

MRS. BIRLING. Careful what you say, dear.

BIRLING *(now at telephone)*. Of course. *(At telephone.)* Brumley eight seven five two. *(To others as he waits.)* I was going to do this anyhow. I've had my suspicions all along. *(At telephone.)* Colonel Roberts, please. Mr. Arthur Birling here. ... Oh, Roberts – Birling here. Sorry to ring you up so late, but can you tell me if an Inspector Goole has joined your staff lately ... Goole. G-O-O-L-E ... a new man ... tall, clean-shaven. *(Here he can describe the appearance of the actor playing the Inspector.)* I see ... yes ... well, that settles it. ... No, just a little argument we were having here.... Good night. *(He puts down the telephone and looks at the others.)* There's no Inspector Goole on the police. That man definitely wasn't a police inspector at all. As Gerald says – we've been had.

MRS. BIRLING. I felt it all the time. He never talked like one. He never even looked like one.

BIRLING. This makes a difference, y'know. In fact, it makes *all* the difference.

GERALD. Of course!

SHEILA *(bitterly)*. I suppose we're all nice people now.

BIRLING. If you've nothing more sensible than that to say, Sheila, you'd better keep quiet.

ERIC. She's right, though.

8 **suspicion:** Verdacht; Mißtrauen.
8f. **all along** (coll.): die ganze Zeit über.
12 **staff:** Belegschaft, Mitarbeiterstab.

BIRLING *(angrily)*. And *you*'d better keep quiet anyhow. If that *had* been a police inspector and he'd heard you confess —

MRS. BIRLING *(warningly)*. Arthur – careful!

BIRLING *(hastily)*. Yes, yes.

SHEILA. You see, Gerald, you haven't to know the rest of our crimes and idiocies.

GERALD. That's all right, I don't want to. *(To Birling.)* What do you make of this business now? Was it a hoax?

BIRLING. Of course. Somebody put that fellow up to coming here and hoaxing us. There are people in this town who dislike me enough to do that. We ought to have seen through it from the first. In the ordinary way, I believe I would have done. But coming like that, bang on top of our little celebration, just when we were all feeling so pleased with ourselves, naturally it took me by surprise.

MRS. BIRLING. I wish I'd been here when that man first arrived. I'd have asked *him* a few questions before I allowed him to ask us any.

SHEILA. It's all right saying that now.

MRS. BIRLING. I was the only one of you who didn't give in to him. And now I say we must discuss this business quietly and sensibly and decide if there's anything to be done about it.

7 **idiocy** (contempt.): Dummheit.
9 **What do you make of ...?:** Was halten Sie von ...?
10 **hoax:** übler Scherz, Streich.
11 **to put s.o. up to s.th.:** jdn. zu etwas anstiften.
12 **to hoax s.o.:** jdm. einen Streich spielen.
15f. **bang on top of:** genau mitten hinein.
23f. **to give in to s.o.:** jdm. nachgeben, sich jdm. geschlagen geben.

BIRLING *(with hearty approval)*. You're absolutely right, my dear. Already we've discovered one important fact – that that fellow was a fraud and we've been hoaxed – and that may not be the end of it by any means.

GERALD. I'm sure it isn't.

BIRLING *(keenly interested)*. You are, eh? Good! *(To Eric, who is restless.)* Eric, sit down.

ERIC *(sulkily)*. I'm all right.

BIRLING. All right? You're anything but all right. And you needn't stand there – as if – as if —

ERIC. As if – what?

BIRLING. As if you'd nothing to do with us. Just remember your own position, young man. If anybody's up to the neck in this business, you are, so you'd better take some interest in it.

ERIC. I do take some interest in it. I take too much, that's my trouble.

SHEILA. It's mine too.

BIRLING. Now listen, you two. If you're still feeling on edge, then the least you can do is to keep quiet. Leave this to us. I'll admit that fellow's antics rattled us a bit. But we've found him out – and all we have to do is to keep our heads. Now it's our turn.

SHEILA. Our turn to do – what?

MRS. BIRLING *(sharply)*. To behave sensibly, Sheila – which is more than you're doing.

ERIC *(bursting out)*. What's the use of talking about behaving sensibly? You're beginning to pretend now

3 **fraud** (coll.): Betrüger, Schwindler.
4 **by any means** (pl.): vielleicht; gar.
19 f. **on edge:** nervös, gereizt.
21 **antics** (pl. fig.): Mätzchen.
to rattle (coll.): nervös machen, durcheinanderbringen.

that nothing's really happened at all. And I can't see it like that. This girl's still dead, isn't she? Nobody's brought her to life, have they?

SHEILA *(eagerly)*. That's just what I feel, Eric. And it's what they don't seem to understand.

ERIC. Whoever that chap was, the fact remains that I did what I did. And Mother did what she did. And the rest of you did what you did to her. It's still the same rotten story whether it's been told to a police inspector or to somebody else. According to you, I ought to feel a lot better — *(To Gerald.)* I stole some money, Gerald, you might as well know — *(As Birling tries to interrupt.)* I don't care, let him know. The money's not the important thing. It's what happened to the girl and what we all did to her that matters. And I still feel the same about it, and that's why I don't feel like sitting down and having a nice cosy talk.

SHEILA. And Eric's absolutely right. And it's the best thing any one of us has said to-night and it makes me feel a bit less ashamed of us. You're just beginning to pretend all over again.

BIRLING. Look – for God's sake!

MRS. BIRLING *(protesting)*. Arthur!

BIRLING. Well, my dear, they're so damned exasperating. They just won't try to understand our position or to see the difference between a lot of stuff like this coming out in private and a downright public scandal.

ERIC *(shouting)*. And I say the girl's dead and we all helped to kill her – and that's what matters —

22 **look:** paß(t) auf!
24 **to exasperate:** wütend machen.
27 **downright:** total, gänzlich.

BIRLING *(also shouting, threatening Eric)*. And I say – either stop shouting or get out. *(Glaring at him but in quiet tone.)* Some fathers I know would have kicked you out of the house anyhow by this time. So hold your tongue if you want to stay here.

ERIC *(quietly, bitterly)*. I don't give a damn now whether I stay here or not.

BIRLING. You'll stay here long enough to give me an account of that money you stole – yes, and to pay it back too.

SHEILA. But that won't bring Eva Smith back to life, will it?

ERIC. And it doesn't alter the fact that we all helped to kill her.

GERALD. But is it a fact?

ERIC. Of course it is. You don't know the whole story yet.

SHEILA. I suppose you're going to prove now you didn't spend last summer keeping this girl instead of seeing me, eh?

GERALD. I did keep a girl last summer. I've admitted it. And I'm sorry, Sheila.

SHEILA. Well, I must admit you came out of it better than the rest of us. The Inspector said that.

BIRLING *(angrily)*. He wasn't an Inspector.

SHEILA *(flaring up)*. Well, he inspected us all right. And don't let's start dodging and pretending now. Between us we drove that girl to commit suicide.

GERALD. Did we? Who says so? Because I say – there's no

6 **not to give a damn** (coll.): keinen Pfifferling darum geben.
8f. **to give s.o. an account of s.th.:** jdm. Rechenschaft über etwas ablegen.
26 **to dodge:** sich drücken, ausweichen.

more real evidence we did than there was that that chap was a police inspector.

SHEILA. Of course there is.

GERALD. No, there isn't. Look at it. A man comes here pretending to be a police officer. It's a hoax of some kind. Now what does he do? Very artfully, working on bits of information he's picked up here and there, he bluffs us into confessing that we've all been mixed up in this girl's life in one way or another.

ERIC. And so we have.

GERALD. *But how do you know it's the same girl?*

BIRLING *(eagerly)*. Now wait a minute! Let's see how that would work. Now — *(hesitates)* no, it wouldn't.

ERIC. We all admitted it.

GERALD. All right, you all admitted something to do with a girl. But how do you know it's the same girl? *(He looks round triumphantly at them. As they puzzle this out, he turns to Birling, after a pause.)* Look here, Mr. Birling. You sack a girl called Eva Smith. You've forgotten, but he shows you a photograph of her and then you remember. Right?

BIRLING. Yes, that part's straightforward enough. But what then?

GERALD. Well, then he happens to know that Sheila once had a girl sacked from Milwards shop. He tells us that it's this same Eva Smith. And he shows her a photograph that she recognises.

SHEILA. Yes. The same photograph.

6 **artfully** (adv.): listig, raffiniert, geschickt.
13 **to work** (fig.): hier: gehen, passen.
17f. **to puzzle s.th. out:** etwas austüfteln, ausknobeln.
22 **straightforward:** einfach, unkompliziert, direkt.

GERALD. How do you know it's the same photograph? Did you see the one your father looked at?

SHEILA. No, I didn't.

GERALD. And did your father see the one he showed you?

SHEILA. No, he didn't. And I see what you mean now.

GERALD. We've no proof it was the same photograph and therefore no proof it was the same girl. Now take me. I never saw a photograph, remember. He caught me out by suddenly announcing that this girl changed her name to Daisy Renton. I gave myself away at once because I'd known a Daisy Renton.

BIRLING *(eagerly)*. And there wasn't the slightest proof that this Daisy Renton was really Eva Smith. We've only his word for it, and we'd his word for it that he was a police inspector, and we know now he was lying. So he could have been lying all the time.

GERALD. Of course he could. Probably was. Now what happened after I left?

MRS. BIRLING. I was upset because Eric had left the house, and this man said that if Eric didn't come back, he'd have to go and find him. Well, that made me feel worse still. And his manner was so severe and he seemed so confident. Then quite suddenly he said I'd seen Eva Smith only two weeks ago.

BIRLING. Those were his exact words.

MRS. BIRLING. And like a fool I said Yes I had.

BIRLING. I don't see now why you did that. She didn't call herself Eva Smith when she came to see you at the committee, did she?

MRS. BIRLING. No, of course she didn't. But, feeling so worried, when he suddenly turned on me with those

8 **to catch s.o. out:** jdn. überführen; auch: ‚erledigen'.

questions, I answered more or less as he wanted me to answer.

SHEILA. But, Mother, don't forget that he showed you a photograph of the girl before that, and you obviously recognised it.

GERALD. Did anybody else see it?

MRS. BIRLING. No, he showed it only to me.

GERALD. Then, don't you see, there's still no proof it was really the same girl. He might have showed you the photograph of any girl who applied to the committee. And how do we know she was really Eva Smith or Daisy Renton?

BIRLING. Gerald's dead right. He could have used a different photograph each time and we'd be none the wiser. We may all have been recognising different girls.

GERALD. Exactly. Did he ask you to identify a photograph, Eric?

ERIC. No. He didn't need a photograph by the time he'd got round to me. But obviously it must have been the girl I knew who went round to see Mother.

GERALD. Why must it?

ERIC. She said she had to have help because she wouldn't take any more stolen money. And the girl I knew had told me that already.

GERALD. Even then, that may have been all nonsense.

ERIC. I don't see much nonsense about it when a girl goes and kills herself. You lot may be letting yourselves out nicely, but I can't. Nor can Mother. We did her in all right.

14 **to be none the wiser:** hier: ohne etwas zu bemerken.
16 **to identify:** identifizieren.
27 **you lot** (coll.): ihr Typen, ihr Leute.
28 **to do s.o. in** (slang): jdn. umbringen, um die Ecke bringen.

BIRLING *(eagerly)*. Wait a minute, wait a minute! Don't be in such a hurry to put yourself into court. That interview with your mother could have been just as much a put-up job, like all this police inspector business. The whole damned thing can have been a piece of bluff.

ERIC *(angrily)*. How can it? The girl's dead, isn't she?

GERALD. What girl? There were probably four or five different girls.

ERIC. That doesn't matter to me. The one I knew is dead.

BIRLING. Is she? *How do we know she is?*

GERALD. That's right. You've got it. How do we know any girl killed herself to-day?

BIRLING *(looking at them all, triumphantly)*. Now answer that one. Let's look at it from this fellow's point of view. We're having a little celebration here and feeling rather pleased with ourselves. Now he has to work a trick on us. Well, the first thing he has to do is to give us such a shock that after that he can bluff us all the time. So he starts right off. A girl has just died in the Infirmary. She drank some strong disinfectant. Died in agony —

ERIC. All right, don't pile it on.

BIRLING *(triumphantly)*. There you are, you see. Just repeating it shakes you a bit. And that's what he had to do. Shake us at once – and then start questioning us – until we didn't know where we were. Oh – let's admit that. He had the laugh of us all right.

4 **a put-up job** (coll.): eine abgekartete Sache, ein Schwindel.
15 **that one:** hier: diese Frage.
28 **to have the laugh of s.o.:** am Ende jdn. auslachen können; am Ende über jdn. triumphieren.

ERIC. He could laugh his head off – if I knew it really was all a hoax.

BIRLING. I'm convinced it is. No police enquiry. No one girl that all this happens to. No scandal —

SHEILA. And no suicide?

GERALD *(decisively)*. We can settle that at once.

SHEILA. How?

GERALD. By ringing up the Infirmary. Either there's a dead girl there or there isn't.

BIRLING *(uneasily)*. It will look a bit queer, won't it – ringing up at this time of night —

GERALD. I don't mind doing it.

MRS. BIRLING *(emphatically)*. And if there isn't —

GERALD. Anyway we'll see. *(He goes to telephone and looks up number. The others watch tensely.)* Brumley eight nine eight six. ... Is that the Infirmary? This is Mr. Gerald Croft – of Crofts Limited. ... Yes. ... We're rather worried about one of our employees. Have you had a girl brought in this afternoon who committed suicide by drinking disinfectant – or any like suicide? Yes, I'll wait.

(As he waits, the others show their nervous tension. Berling wipes his brow, Sheila shivers, Eric clasps and unclasps his hands, etc.)

Yes? ... You're certain of that. ... I see. Well, thank you very much. ... Good night. *(He puts down telephone and looks at them.)* No girl has died in there to-

13 **emphatically** (adv.): nachdrücklich, eindringlich.
15 **tensely** (adv.): (an)gespannt; verkrampft.
22 **tension:** (An-)Spannung.
23 **to shiver:** zittern.
23f. **to clasp one's hands:** die Hände (fest) ineinanderpressen.

day. Nobody's been brought in after drinking disinfectant. They haven't had a suicide for months.

BIRLING *(triumphantly)*. There you are! Proof positive. The whole story's just a lot of moonshine. Nothing but an elaborate sell! *(He produces a huge sigh of relief.)* Nobody likes to be sold as badly as that – but – for all that – *(he smiles at them all)* Gerald, have a drink.

GERALD *(smiling)*. Thanks, I think I could just do with one now.

BIRLING *(going to sideboard)*. So could I.

MRS. BIRLING *(smiling)*. And I must say, Gerald, you've argued this very cleverly, and I'm most grateful.

GERALD *(going for his drink)*. Well, you see, while I was out of the house I'd time to cool off and think things out a little.

BIRLING *(giving him a drink)*. Yes, he didn't keep you on the run as he did the rest of us. I'll admit now he gave me a bit of a scare at the time. But I'd a special reason for not wanting any public scandal just now. *(Has his drink now, and raises his glass.)* Well, here's to us. Come on, Sheila, don't look like that. All over now.

SHEILA. The worst part is. But you're forgetting one thing I still can't forget. Everything we said had happened really had happened. If it didn't end tragically, then that's lucky for us. But it might have done.

4 **moonshine** (fig.): Unsinn; Schwindel.
5 **sell** (coll.): Schwindel, Betrug.
6f. **for all that:** trotz alledem.
12 **to argue:** beweisen; hier auch: machen.
14 **to cool off** (coll.): sich beruhigen.
16f. **to keep s.o. on the run:** jdn. auf Trab halten.
20 **here's to us:** auf unser Wohl! Prosit!

BIRLING *(jovially)*. But the whole thing's different now. Come, come, you can see that, can't you? *(Imitating Inspector in his final speech.) You all helped to kill her. (Pointing at Sheila and Eric, and laughing.)* And I wish you could have seen the look on your faces when he said that. *(Sheila moves towards door.)* Going to bed, young woman?

SHEILA *(tensely)*. I want go get out of this. It frightens me the way you talk.

BIRLING *(heartily)*. Nonsense! You'll have a good laugh over it yet. Look, you'd better ask Gerald for that ring you gave back to him, hadn't you? Then you'll feel better.

SHEILA *(passionately)*. You're pretending everything's just as it was before.

ERIC. I'm not!

SHEILA. No, but these others are.

BIRLING. Well, isn't it? We've been had, that's all.

SHEILA. So nothing really happened. So there's nothing to be sorry for, nothing to learn. We can all go on behaving just as we did.

MRS. BIRLING. Well, why shouldn't we?

SHEILA. I tell you – whoever that Inspector was, it was anything but a joke. You knew it then. You began to learn something. And now you've stopped. You're ready to go on in the same old way.

BIRLING *(amused)*. And you're not, eh?

SHEILA. No, because I remember what he said, how he looked, and what he made me feel. Fire and blood and anguish. And it frightens me the way you talk, and I can't listen to any more of it.

1 **jovially** (adv.): fröhlich, vergnügt.

ERIC. And I agree with Sheila. It frightens me too.

BIRLING. Well, go to bed then, and don't stand there being hysterical.

MRS. BIRLING. They're over-tired. In the morning they'll be as amused as we are.

GERALD. Everything's all right now, Sheila. *(Holds up the ring.)* What about this ring?

SHEILA. No, not yet. It's too soon. I must think.

BIRLING *(pointing to Eric and Sheila)*. Now look at the pair of them – the famous younger generation who know it all. And they can't even take a joke —

(The telephone rings sharply. There is a moment's complete silence. Birling goes to answer it.)

Yes? ... Mr. Birling speaking ... *What?* – Here —

(But obviously the other person has rung off. He puts the telephone down slowly and looks in a panic-stricken fashion at the others.)

BIRLING. That was the police. A girl has just died – on her way to the Infirmary – after swallowing some disinfectant. And a police inspector is on his way here – to ask some – questions —

(As they stare guiltily and dumbfounded, the curtain falls.)

15 **to ring off:** den Hörer auflegen.
16 **panic-stricken:** mit panischem Schrecken erfüllt.
22 **dumbfounded:** verblüfft, sprachlos.

Editorische Notiz

Der englische Text folgt der Ausgabe: *The Plays of J. B. Priestley*, Bd. 3, London: Heinemann, 1950. Das Glossar erklärt in der Regel alle Wörter, die über die Wertigkeitsstufe 4 des *Englischen Arbeitswörterbuches* von Alfred Haase (Frankfurt a. M.: Moritz Diesterweg, [7]1979) hinausgehen. Im Zweifelsfall wurde großzügig verfahren, d. h. eher eine Vokabel mehr aufgenommen als dort vorgesehen.

Im Glossar verwendete Abkürzungen

adv.	adverb
coll.	colloquial (umgangssprachlich)
contempt.	contemptuously (verächtlich)
fig.	figuratively (übertragen)
jur.	jurisprudence (bei Ausdrücken aus der Rechtssprache)
lat.	lateinisch
o.s.	oneself
pl.	plural
s.o.	someone
s.th.	something

Anmerkungen

1 »Old Vic« bedeutet hier die Old Vic Theatre Company, die in der Royal Victorian Hall zu Hause war, aber auch zu Theateraufführungen in Orte außerhalb Londons und ins Ausland reiste. Nachdem die Uraufführung des Stückes in russischer Übersetzung im Sommer des Jahres 1945 in Moskau stattgefunden hatte, wurde die erste Aufführung im heimischen London von Basil Dean besorgt – und zwar im Oktober 1946 im New Theatre. Das Ensemble bestand aus hervorragenden Schauspielern und Schauspielerinnen, dem z. B. auch der spätere weltberühmte Sir Alec Guinness angehörte, der die Rolle des Eric Birling spielte.

2 Der Ausdruck geht zurück auf einen Befehl an die Soldaten des East Kent Regiments, das als Beinamen »The Buffs« führte – wegen der ledergelben Farbe der Uniformaufschläge.

3 Gemeint ist hier der letzte deutsche Kaiser Wilhelm II. (1859–1941), der von 1888 bis 1918 regierte und der wegen seines »Säbelrasselns« vor allem im europäischen Ausland nicht unwesentlich für eine politisch-militärische Unruhe gegenüber dem deutschen Kaiserreich sorgte.

4 Die »Titanic« war mit 46329 BRT das größte und modernste Passagierschiff der damaligen Zeit. Auf ihrer Jungfernreise von Southampton nach New York stieß sie in der Nacht des 14. April 1912 mit einem Eisberg zusammen und sank, obwohl sie durch eine neuartige Konstruktion als unsinkbar gegolten hatte. Mehr als 1500 Menschen kamen dabei ums Leben. Im Sommer des Jahres 1986 versuchte eine US-amerikanische Expedition das inzwischen entdeckte Wrack zu untersuchen und zu bergen.

5 Mit dem Gegensatzpaar »Kapital« (bzw. Besitzer von »Produktionsmitteln«) und »Arbeit« wird auf den ökonomisch-sozialen Grundkonflikt angespielt, so wie er von Karl Marx (*Das Kapital*, erschienen 1867–1910) gesehen und beschrieben wurde.

6 George Bernard Shaw (1856–1950), bedeutender geistvoll-witziger Dramatiker, und Herbert George Wells (1866 bis 1946), produktiver rationalistischer Schriftsteller, engagieren sich beide ungemein stark für Sozialreformen und üben in ihren Arbeiten scharfe Kritik an den gesellschaftlichen Zuständen der Zeit.

7 Auf Vorschlag des jeweiligen Premierministers verleiht die britische Königin (bzw. der König) regelmäßig zweimal im Jahr Adelstitel und Orden an ausgewählte Persönlichkeiten. Jeweils zum offiziellen Geburtstag der Monarchin und zu Neujahr wird diese sogenannte »Honours List« veröffentlicht.

8 Anspielung auf die traditionelle Erziehung der männlichen Mitglieder der vornehmen englischen Gesellschaft mit teurer Internats- und anschließender Universitätsausbildung – möglichst in den Eliteuniversitäten Oxford oder Cambridge.

9 »Magistrates« (in der Regel auch »Justices of the Peace«) sind Laienrichter, die minder schwere Kriminalfälle rechtskräftig aburteilen können, d. h. bis zu £ 400 an Geldstrafe oder bis zu 6 Monaten an Gefängnisstrafe verhängen dürfen. Im sogenannten »Magistrates' Court«, der wöchentlich mindestens zweimal tagt, sind diese ehrenamtlichen Richter tätig, die sich in ihrem Umfeld zumeist allgemeiner Hochachtung erfreuen. Juristisch beraten werden sie von qualifizierten Anwälten, den »Clerks«. Fälle, die die Kompetenzen der »Magistrates' Courts« übersteigen, werden an höhere Gerichte überwiesen. In London und in anderen Großstädten gibt es heute allerdings auch »magistrates«, die als Berufsrichter mit entsprechender juristischer Ausbildung arbeiten. Sie dürfen sich jedoch nicht – wohl um die Laienrichter nicht zu diskreditieren – »judges« nennen. Vgl. auch in diesem Zusammenhang den Ausdruck »to be on the Bench«, S. 18).

10 Londoner Wohnsitz der britischen Könige und Königinnen.

11 In diesen Frauenvereinigungen, die zumeist sozial bzw. karitativ ausgerichtet waren, wurden allerdings in der Regel nur

die Ehefrauen gesellschaftlich führender Persönlichkeiten als Mitglieder aufgenommen. Diese Frauen pflegten in ganz besonderem Maße die offiziellen moralischen Maßstäbe – nach außen – zu verkörpern und gleichzeitig rigoros zu überwachen. Die tatsächlich geleisteten Hilfen für sogenannte »fallen women« verstärkte natürlich andererseits die (z. T. heuchlerische) Meinung und den Anspruch dieser Frauen, selbst moralisch unantastbar zu sein.

Literaturhinweise

Atkins, J., *J. B. Priestley. The Last of the Sages*, London / New York 1981.

Braine, J., *J. B. Priestley*, London 1978.

Brown, I., *J. B. Priestley*, erw. Neuaufl. London 1964 (Writers and Their Work 84).

Cooper, S., *J. B. Priestley. Portrait of an Author*, London 1970.

Dotzenrath, T., »Priestleys *An Inspector Calls* als Schullektüre«, in: *Die Neueren Sprachen* 10 (1956) S. 480–484.

Evans, G. L., *J. B. Priestley. The Dramatist*, London 1964.

Fricker, R., *Das moderne englische Drama*, Göttingen 1964, S. 70–74.

Fuchs, K., »J. B. Priestley«, in: *Die Neueren Sprachen* 5 (1966) S. 221–226.

Goetsch, P., »Das englische Drama seit Shaw«, in: J. Nünning (Hrsg.), *Das englische Drama*, Darmstadt 1973, S. 403–507, bes. S. 420 ff.

Heybey, W., »John B. Priestley, *Ein Inspektor kommt*«, in: *Reclam Lesestoffe – Lehrpraktische Analysen*, Folge 7, Stuttgart 1958, S. 23–31.

Hortmann, W., *Englische Literatur im 20. Jahrhundert*, Bern / München 1965, S. 123 f., 153 f.

Hughes, D., *J. B. Priestley. An Informal Study of his Work*, London 1958.

Löb, L., *Mensch und Gesellschaft bei J. B. Priestley*, Winterthur/Bern 1962 (Schweizer Anglistische Arbeiten, 53).

Lumley, F., *New Trends in 20th Century Drama*, London 1967.

Maack, A., »Dramatiker der Vorkriegszeit im englischen Theater nach 1945«, in: H. Kosok (Hrsg.), *Drama und Theater im England des 20. Jahrhunderts*, Düsseldorf 1980, S. 105–115.

MacRae, D. G., *The World of J. B. Priestley*, London 1967.

Oetting, W., »J. B. Priestley, *An Inspector Calls*. Eine Erörterung des Schauspielschlusses«, in: *Die Neueren Sprachen* 11 (1966) S. 535–539.

Peinert, D., »J. B. Priestley, *An Inspector Calls*. Wege und

Irrwege zur Interpretation des Dramas«, in: *Praxis des neusprachlichen Unterrichts* 4 (1966) S 333–346.

Poppe, R., *Erläuterungen zu John Boynton Priestley »Ein Inspektor kommt«*, Hollfeld 1982.

Roth, W., »Priestley, J. B., *An Inspector Calls*«, in: J. V. Hagopian / M. Dolch (Hrsg.), *Insight II*, Frankfurt a. M. [3]1970, S. 293–302.

Schlösser, A., »A Critical Survey of Some of Priestley's Plays«, in: *Zeitschrift für Anglistik und Amerikanistik* 2 (1962) S. 131–142.

Schirmer, W. F., *Geschichte der englischen und amerikanischen Literatur*, Bd. 2, Tübingen [3]1960, S. 250 f., 295.

Young, K., *J. B. Priestley*, London 1977 (Writers and Their Work, 257).

Nachtrag 2003

Coleman, R., *A Guide to »An Inspector Calls«*, London 1999 (Teach Yourself Revision Guides: English Literature Guides).

Gooden, Ph., *Brodie's Notes on J. B. Priestley's »An Inspector Calls«*, London 1996.

Gray, D., *J. B. Priestley*, Stroud 2000 (Sutton Pocket Biographies).

Klein, H. M., *J. B. Priestley's Plays*, London 1998.

Kröger, H., *J. B. Priestley, »An Inspector Calls«. Unterrichtsmodell*, Paderborn 2000 (EinFach Englisch).

Linde, H. van de, »*An Inspector Calls* – Vorschläge für einen *active approach* in der Jahrgangsstufe 11«, in: *Der Fremdsprachliche Unterricht – Englisch* 27 (1993) H. 10, S. 36–40.

Mahoney, J., *J. B. Priestley, »An Inspector Calls«*, London 1994 (Letts Explore for GCSE).

Meyer, H., *J. B. Priestley, »An Inspector Calls«*, Stuttgart 1996 (Teacher's Guide).

Real, W., *J. B. Priestley, »An Inspector Calls«*, München 1995 (Lehrerhandreichungen).

Scicluna, J., *J. B. Priestley, »An Inspector Calls«*, London 1997 (York Notes for GSCE).
– *J. B. Priestley, »An Inspector Calls«*, London 2002 (York Notes).
Ulm, D., *J. B. Priestley, »An Inspector Calls«*, Freising 2001 (Interpretationshilfe Englisch).

Nachwort

I

Als John Boynton Priestley am 14. August 1984 fast neunzigjährig in seinem Haus in Alveston bei Stratford-on-Avon starb, war ein langes, außerordentlich produktives und farbiges Schriftstellerleben zu Ende gegangen. Priestley, der bereits als Neunzehnjähriger zu veröffentlichen begonnen hatte, war im wahrsten Sinne des Wortes ein »all-round writer«[1]. Zu seinem Mammutwerk gehören: Kritiken, Essays, Romane, Erzählungen, Kurzgeschichten, Reiseberichte, Dramen, Gedichte, Autobiographisches, Drehbücher, Hörspiele und sogar ein Opernlibretto. Allein über einhundert eigenständige Publikationen werden z. B. in der Ausgabe von 1984 des *Who's Who* unter seinem Namen aufgeführt.[2]

Betrachten wir nun diesen so erstaunlich aktiven Mann und sein vielfältiges literarisches Schaffen etwas näher. Dabei gilt es von vornherein, sich der Tatsache bewußt zu bleiben, daß das Werk eines derart produktiven Autors naturgemäß in künstlerischer Hinsicht sehr ungleich ausfallen muß, so daß Arbeiten, die mehr für den Tag geschrieben sind, neben solchen stehen, die sich dem zeitlos Gültigen nähern. Ferner sei darauf hingewiesen, daß Priestley die für seine geistige und moralische Haltung entscheidenden und lebenslang richtungweisenden Prägungen zum einen durch sein Elternhaus erhielt, zum anderen durch die soziokulturelle Situation in seiner Heimatstadt Bradford und schließlich durch die Erfahrungen im Ersten Weltkrieg.[3]

John Boynton Priestley wurde am 13. September 1894 in der nordenglischen Industriestadt Bradford geboren. Sein Vater, Jonathan Priestley, ein der Arbeiterschaft entstammender Lehrer und späterer Rektor einer Grundschule, war ein warmherzi-

1 So Ivor Brown; zit. nach: L. Löb, *Mensch und Gesellschaft bei J. B. Priestley*, Winterthur / Bern 1962, S. 2.

2 Vgl. *Who's Who*, London 1984, S. 1846 f.

3 Wir folgen hier weitgehend den Ausführungen von J. Braine, *J. B. Priestley*, London 1978, S. 7–18.

ger, christlich geprägter Sozialist, der z. B. als einer der ersten die Schulspeisung in der Grundschule einführte. Obwohl seine Mutter früh verstarb und sein Vater wieder heiratete, verlebte Priestley insgesamt eine glückliche Kindheit in einer gemäßigt sozialistischen Atmosphäre mit einem gewissen kulturellen Niveau, für das die reichlich gefüllten »bookshelves and piano«[4] sichtbarer Ausdruck waren. Priestley besuchte mit gutem Erfolg die Belle Vue Grammar School in Bradford, ging aber – weil er schulmüde war und ohnehin nicht studieren wollte – als Sechzehnjähriger von der Schule ab und trat als »junior clerk« in eine Wollfirma seiner Heimatstadt ein. Die Büroarbeit langweilte ihn schrecklich, um so mehr genoß er in seiner Freizeit, was die Stadt ihm kulturell zu bieten hatte: »He stowed himself into the cheaper seats at theatres, he visited music halls [...], he attended Arts clubs and Playgoers' societies [...].«[5] In dieser Zeit begann Priestley Artikel zu schreiben – vor allem für die örtliche Parteizeitung *Bradford Pioneer*, »a Bradford Labour weekly«[6] – durchaus schon mit dem Ziel, einmal als Schriftsteller sein Brot zu verdienen.

Das reiche kulturelle Angebot der Stadt wirkte ebenso prägend auf Priestley wie die hier erfahrene fortschrittliche Aufgeschlossenheit im sozialen Bereich. »Bradford was progressive and alive, a reforming city, a pioneering city. It was not only the city in which e v e r y bright boy or girl had a chance of a grammar school education, it was also the city in which Margaret Macmillan set up her first school for handicapped children. It was the cradle of the Independent Labour Party, it was a powerhouse of social change.«[7]

Im September 1914 meldete sich Priestley freiwillig zur Armee. Er diente zunächst in The Duke of Wellington's West Riding Regiment und schließlich ab 1918 als Offizier im Devonshire Regiment. Er wurde als Frontsoldat in Frankreich zweimal verwundet und mußte mit ansehen, wie viele seiner Kameraden

4 Vgl. S. Cooper, *J. B. Priestley. Portrait of an Author*, London 1970, S. 12.

5 K. Young, *J. B. Priestley*, London 1977, S. 9.

6 Braine, S. 13.

7 Braine, S. 15 (Hervorhebung vom Hrsg.).

starben. Verbittert und entsetzt verließ er 1919 als Fünfundzwanzigjähriger die Armee, nicht zuletzt auch wegen dieser Erfahrung: »During the war [...] he first encountered the English class system. The army he joined was commanded by English gentlemen – gentlemen first, officers a long way after – who combined impenetrable stupidity with impenetrable complacency.«[8]

Mit einem bescheidenen Stipendium für ehemalige Armeeangehörige studierte Priestley sodann an der renommierten Universität Cambridge (Trinity Hall) Literaturwissenschaften, Geschichte und Politik. Inzwischen mit der ehemaligen Nachbarstochter Pat Tempest verheiratet (1919), ging Priestley nach Beendigung seines Studiums im Jahre 1922 als Achtundzwanzigjähriger nach London, um sich dort als freier Schriftsteller niederzulassen. Sein Startkapital waren £ 50 und eine 1922 erschienene, erste Buchveröffentlichung *Brief Diversions* – eine Sammlung von Essays und Parodien.

Bis J. B. Priestley mit der Veröffentlichung seines siebzehnten Buches und vierten Romans, *The Good Companions* (1929), der Durchbruch gelang und er damit auch den Grundstein zu einer Art dauerhafter materieller Sicherheit legen konnte, hatte er sich bereits einen Namen als einfühlsamer Kritiker und insbesondere als geistreicher Essayist gemacht.[9] Der Erfolgsroman *The Good Companions* brachte Priestley allerdings auch den lebenslang weiter nachwirkenden Vorwurf ein, unter Aufgabe eines künstlerischen Anspruches bewußt für ein Millionenpublikum zu schreiben, was u. a. dazu führte, daß ihn die etablierte akademische Literaturkritik eigentlich nie ernstgenommen und angemessen gewürdigt hat.[10]

Unbeeindruckt von dieser Kritik setzte Priestley seine breite schriftstellerische Tätigkeit fort, und mit dem Roman *Angel*

8 Braine, S. 16.

9 Zu nennen sind hier z. B. seine Darstellungen über *George Meredith* (1926), *Thomas Love Peacock* (1927) oder über *The English Novel* (1927) sowie die Essaybände *Talking* (1926) und *Apes and Angels* (1928).

10 Vgl. etwa Löb, S. 10, und Braine, S. 26. In diesem Zusammenhang muß auch auf Priestleys ironisch-abwertenden Spitznamen »Jolly Jack« hingewiesen werden.

Pavement (1930) erzielte er einen zweiten Riesenerfolg. Typisch für all seine Romane ist, daß er – in der Tradition von Henry Fielding und Charles Dickens stehend – das Alltagsleben der »kleinen Leute« mit ihren romantischen Sehnsüchten darstellt. Seine liebevoll-realistischen Genrebilder und humorvollen Charakterschilderungen, aber auch der klare Handlungsablauf und die einfach-plastische Sprache sind Ausdruck einer erdverbundenen und lebensbejahenden Einstellung, der freilich auch die Konfrontation mit vielfältigen menschlichen Enttäuschungen und insbesondere z. T. scharfe Sozialkritik nicht fremd sind.

Nach diesen Publikumserfolgen stellte sich Priestley bewußt einer neuen schriftstellerischen Herausforderung: nämlich der, Theaterstücke zu schreiben. Gleich sein erstes eigenes Stück, *Dangerous Corner* (1932), wurde ein Bühnenerfolg.[11] Priestleys Tätigkeit als Dramatiker kann – neben seinem Wirken als Essayist und als Romancier – als eine Art dritter Schwerpunkt in seinem literarischen Schaffen angesehen werden.

Wie bisher schrieb und publizierte Priestley ununterbrochen weiter – und damit nicht genug, er beteiligte sich auch aktiv am Theatermanagement (London Mask Theatre) und an der Produktion seiner Theaterstücke in London und New York, allerdings mit wechselndem Erfolg. Längere Arbeitsaufenthalte in den USA (im Staat Arizona und in der Filmstadt Hollywood) fallen ebenfalls in diese dreißiger Jahre. Das Jahr 1937 brachte mit den beiden Bühnenstücken *Time and the Conways* und *I Have Been Here Before* neue Erfolge – insbesondere auch deshalb, weil Priestley hier äußerst bühnenwirksam mit der Durchbrechung der Chronologie experimentiert. Auf diese Weise gelingt es ihm, seelische Vorgänge in neuartiger Form bewußt zu machen und seine dramatischen Absichten sehr eindrucksvoll zu verwirklichen.[12]

11 Im Jahr 1931 hatte er zusammen mit Edward Knoblock eine Dramenfassung seines Romans *The Good Companions* herausgebracht.

12 Anregungen bezüglich der »Zeit-Problematik« erhielt Priestley durch die Lektüre insbesondere folgender Bücher: J. W. Dunne, *An Experiment with Time*, London 1927, und P. D. Ouspensky, *A New Model of the Universe*, London 1931.

Seit seinem ersten Erfolgsstück im Jahre 1932 schrieb Priestley bis zum Ausbruch des Zweiten Weltkrieges im Jahre 1939 insgesamt fünfzehn Theaterstücke. Sie zeichnen sich stets durch packende Handlung und lebendigen Dialog aus und bringen meist Schicksale einfacher Menschen auf die Bühne, wobei sehr geschickt ethische bzw. politisch-weltanschauliche Positionen dramatisch umgesetzt werden.
Während des Zweiten Weltkrieges – von 1940 bis 1941 – errang Priestley mit seinen zehnminütigen sonntäglichen Radiosendungen (Postscripts) nach den Neun-Uhr-Nachrichten eine ungeheure Popularität im ganzen Land. Es waren im Grunde genommen sehr persönlich gehaltene »gesprochene Essays« über Alltäglichkeiten, aber sie erreichten tiefe Schichten der ums Überleben kämpfenden britischen Nation. Vierzehn Bücher ganz unterschiedlicher Art wurden von Priestley in den Kriegsjahren veröffentlicht.
Nach dem Kriege entstanden mit *An Inspector Calls* (1945), *The Linden Tree* (1947) und *Summer Day's Dream* (1949) Theaterstücke, in denen Priestley insbesondere seiner Einstellung zu einem humanen Sozialismus anschaulich Ausdruck verlieh. Aber auch z. B. mit den Romanen *Three Men in New Suits* (1945), *Jenny Villiers* (1947) oder mit den Reisebildern *Journey Down a Rainbow* (1955) gelang es Priestley in dieser Nachkriegsepoche, sein sozialkritisches Anliegen unmißverständlich und nachhaltig zu Gehör zu bringen.
Neben seinen schriftstellerischen Tätigkeiten nahm J. B. Priestley auch noch eine ganze Reihe administrativer bzw. repräsentativer Aufgaben wahr: so vor allem von 1946 bis 1947 als britischer Delegierter bei der UNESCO, als Vorsitzender und Mitglied nationaler und internationaler Theatergesellschaften und anderer Berufsverbände. Ferner war Priestley zusammen mit dem Philosophen Bertrand Russell Begründer der Kampagne für atomare Abrüstung (CND) und setzte sich öffentlich mit Engagement gegen die Todesstrafe, Umweltverschmutzung oder die »Vermassung«[13] ein.

13 Vgl. in diesem Zusammenhang seine bekannte Wortschöpfung »Admass« – zur Bezeichnung der Auswüchse des auf kurzlebige Massenproduktion ausgerichteten amerikanischen Wirtschaftssystems.

Von seinen späten Veröffentlichungen verdienen sein längster Roman *The Image Men* (zweiteilig, 1968/69) und als eine Art letzter Schwerpunkt seine sozialgeschichtlichen Arbeiten wie *The Edwardians* (1970), *Victoria's Heyday* (1972) oder *The English* (1973) besondere Erwähnung.

Aufschlußreiche Einblicke in sein Leben und Schaffen gewährte J. B. Priestley mit seinen autobiographischen Schriften *Midnight on the Desert* (1937), *Rain upon Godshill* (1939), *Margin Released* (1962) und *Instead of the Trees* (1977).

Priestley, der Ehrungen und Preisen relativ ablehnend gegenüberstand, hat in seinem Leben nur sehr wenige Auszeichnungen angenommen: so z. B. die Ehrenbürgerwürde seiner Vaterstadt Bradford (1973) oder die ihm von der Königin im Jahre 1977 verliehene höchste britische Auszeichnung, den »Order of Merit« (OM).

Nach dem frühen Krebstod seiner ersten Frau, mit der Priestley zwei Kinder hatte, heiratete er 1926 Jane Wyndham Lewis, die eine Tochter mit in die Ehe brachte. Aus dieser Verbindung gingen drei Kinder hervor. Im Jahre 1952 erfolgte die Trennung, und ein Jahr später heiratete Priestley ein drittes Mal: die Archäologin und Schriftstellerin Jacquetta Hawkes, mit der er auch gemeinsam etliche Bücher veröffentlichte.

J. B. Priestleys politisch-weltanschauliche Position, die sein ganzes literarisches Schaffen mehr oder weniger deutlich bestimmt und die sich in erster Linie an jenen prägenden Erfahrungen orientiert, die er in seinem Elternhaus, in seiner Heimatstadt Bradford und im Ersten Weltkrieg machte, läßt sich mit dem Begriff »liberaler Sozialismus«[14] einigermaßen zutreffend beschreiben. Kurz gesagt ist damit gemeint, daß ein wirklich befriedigendes Dasein sich frei entfaltender menschlicher Individuen nur in einer gerechten und brüderlichen Gemeinschaft möglich ist. Priestley prangert deshalb alle antisozialen Haltungen an, insbesondere Habgier und rücksichtsloses Machtstreben. In seinen besten Arbeiten gelingt es ihm, seine Botschaft in solche Formen zu kleiden, daß Leben und Idee,

14 So Löb. S. 7.

Kunst und Predigt zu einer harmonischen Einheit mit großer Suggestivkraft verschmelzen und sich so über den Tag hinaus zu einer eindrucksvollen Darstellung von menschlichen Grunderfahrungen und Verhaltensweisen verdichten.

II

Das Erfolgsstück *An Inspector Calls* schrieb Priestley im Winter 1944/45 in nur einer Woche. Obwohl es – vordergründig betrachtet – durch die Aufklärung der Verstrickung der Hauptpersonen in ein Tötungsdelikt als *detective play* angesehen werden könnte, ist es doch sehr viel zutreffender als eine »moderne Moralität« oder als *problem play* im konventionell-gesellschaftlichen Rahmen der *comedy of manners* oder aber auch als eine Art Vorläufer des *social drama* der fünfziger Jahre anzusprechen. Zwar lassen sowohl der realistisch gezeichnete äußere Rahmen als auch das Handlungsgeschehen selbst – insbesondere die angewandte analytische Aufklärungstechnik – zunächst an ein *detective play* denken, in dem es um die mehr oder minder spannend-unterhaltsame Klärung eines Kriminalfalles geht, aber bei einer näheren Betrachtung wird schnell deutlich, daß Priestley hier etwas anderes als bloße Unterhaltung beabsichtigt, daß er vielmehr bewußt Elemente dieser publikumswirksamen Form benutzt, um ein bestimmtes Anliegen, seine *message*, nachdrücklich zum Ausdruck zu bringen. Die Verstöße gegen die »wirklichkeitsbezogene Glaubwürdigkeit«[15], d. h. gegen die naturgetreue Abbildung der Realität, sind denn auch ein eindeutiges Indiz gegen ein reines *detective play*, für das gerade die logisch verknüpfte Abfolge realer Lebenssituationen wesentliche Grundbedingung ist. Auch der Ort der Handlung, Brumley, eine fiktive Stadt, die vom Lautbild her Assoziationen zu den Industriestädten Birmingham, Bradford und Burnley erweckt, spricht gegen eine Verankerung des Stückes in der Realität. Priestley will damit deutlich

15 D. Peinert, »J. B. Priestley, *An Inspector Calls*. Wege und Irrwege zur Interpretation des Dramas«, in: *Praxis des neusprachlichen Unterrichts* 4 (1966) S. 335.

machen, daß sein Theaterstück in einer typischen englischen Industriestadt spielt, die überall sein könnte, d. h. er hebt die engen Grenzen lokalisierbarer Räumlichkeit auf und läßt bereits so sein Stück in den Bereich des Allgemeingültigen vorstoßen. Als weitere Verstöße gegen die »wirklichkeitsbezogene Glaubwürdigkeit« können beispielsweise die folgenden Gegebenheiten gelten: tatsächlich sind alle Familienmitglieder unabhängig voneinander für den Tod ein und desselben Menschen mitverantwortlich; ferner stellt hier ein Inspektor Nachforschungen an, obwohl es sich eindeutig um einen Todesfall ohne fremdes Verschulden handelt, und schließlich wird durch den effektvollen, aber realitätsfremden Anruf am Ende des Stückes suggeriert, daß nunmehr noch eine echte polizeiliche Untersuchung des Selbstmordfalles stattfinden wird.

Wenn man außerdem bedenkt, daß auch die Hauptfiguren selbst nicht so sehr als charakteristische Einzelpersönlichkeiten, sondern stärker als »zeittypische Erscheinungen« in einer bestimmten gesellschaftlichen Situation[16] angelegt sind, worauf z. B. schon die Namen Birling (Klangassoziation zu *burly* ›kräftig‹ und zu *sterling* ›Sterling‹ [brit. Währung; Geld]) und vor allem Eva Smith (sprechender Name als Hinweis auf die Vertreterin der Mitmenschen schlechthin) deutlich hinweisen,[17] dann wird ganz offensichtlich, daß es Priestley darum geht, dem »Kriminalfall Birling« eine allgemeingültige Dimension zu geben.

Was ist Priestleys Anliegen? Es ist die Widerlegung des »kapitalistischen Glaubensbekenntnisses«[18] von Mr. Birling, der am Ende der Exposition seine Lebensphilosophie folgendermaßen formuliert: »[...] community and all that nonsense. [...] a man has to mind his own business and look after himself and his own –« (S. 17). Der »Polizeiinspektor Goole« kann am Ende des Verhörs, das die moralische Schuld aller Familienangehöri-

16 Vgl. W. Heybey, »John B. Priestley, *Ein Inspektor kommt*«, in: *Reclam Lesestoffe – Lehrpraktische Analysen*, Folge 7, Stuttgart 1958, S. 24.

17 Vgl. W. Roth, »Priestley, J. B., *An Inspector Calls*«, in: J. V. Hagopian / M. Dolch (Hrsg.), *Insight II*, Frankfurt a. M. ³1970, S. 301, und T. Dotzenrath, »Priestleys *An Inspector Calls* als Schullektüre«, in: *Die Neueren Sprachen* 10 (1956) S. 480.

18 Vgl. Roth, S. 295, der den Begriff »capitalist creed« benutzt.

gen offenlegt, um so wirkungsvoller seine Gegenposition – d. h. Priestleys moralische Forderung – vortragen: »One Eva Smith has gone – but there are millions and millions and millions of Eva Smiths and John Smiths still left with us [. . .]. We don't live alone. We are members of one body. We are responsible for each other« (S. 77).

Doch wer befolgt diesen moralischen Appell? Die Reaktionen der Familienmitglieder nach dem Weggang von Inspektor Goole zeigen, daß nur Eric und Sheila bereit sind, die moralischen Forderungen ernst zu nehmen – trotz der Konsequenzen, die der Inspektor bei ihrer Nichtbeachtung ankündigt. Im Hinblick auf die Befolgung dieses Appells an das soziale Gewissen ist Priestley also eher pessimistisch, wenngleich auch die hoffnungsvollen Anzeichen nicht übersehen werden sollen, die sich charakteristischerweise bei Vertretern der jungen Generation zeigen.

Immer wieder hat die Beantwortung zweier Fragen gewisse Schwierigkeiten bereitet, vor allem bei einer mehr inhaltsbezogenen bzw. werkimmanenten Interpretation des Stückes: Wer oder was ist dieser Polizeiinspektor Goole und was soll der Telefonanruf am Ende des Stückes?

Goole, für den Priestley bezeichnenderweise kaum individualisierende Merkmale bereithält, ist nicht als eigenständige Person von Interesse, sondern dient nur als die bühnengerechte Möglichkeit, zum einen die äußere, spannende Handlung voranzutreiben und zum anderen als Sprachrohr für Priestleys soziales Anliegen zu fungieren. Man kann ihn zutreffend als das »personifizierte Gewissen der Schuldigen, als die ›innere Stimme‹«[19] oder auch als die Verkörperung des Kollektivgewissens ansehen, dem nichts Überirdisches anhaftet.

Der Telefonanruf am Ende des Stückes kann nicht sinnvoll als ein reales Ereignis aufgefaßt, sondern muß vielmehr als eindrucksvolles dramaturgisches Mittel verstanden werden. Mitten hinein in das wiedererlangte Hochgefühl von Selbstsicherheit und Selbstgefälligkeit platzt dieser Anruf und macht schlag-

19 Heybey, S. 26.

artig klar, »daß ein Ausweichen vor der Forderung des Inspektors unmöglich ist.«[20] Er gibt dem sozialen Appell des Inspektors einen ungeheuren Nachdruck, indem er suggeriert, daß das ganze Geschehen mit den uns bereits bekannten »Ergebnissen« sich nochmals, aber nunmehr in der Realität abspielen wird. Durch den Schock, den der Telefonanruf bei den Familienmitgliedern auslöst, wird sowohl ihre angstvolle Betroffenheit verdeutlicht als auch das soziale Anliegen des Stückes als bedrükkend realistisch und dringlich unterstrichen.

An Inspector Calls – ist ein zeitlos gültiger A u f r u f in Dramenform an uns alle, uns um unsere Mitmenschen zu kümmern. Das Stück ist die erschreckend eindringliche Darstellung des Gedankens, daß eine Gesellschaft, in der es nur darum geht, rücksichtslos egoistische Interessen durchzusetzen, inhuman ist. Es ist aber auch ein treffend gezeichnetes Zeitbild der wohlhabenden bürgerlichen Gesellschaft vor dem Ersten Weltkrieg, deren Meinungen und Verhaltensweisen – wie z. B. unkritischer Fortschrittsglaube, Profitstreben, doppelte Moral usw. – scharf kritisiert werden. »Mit seiner exakt eingefangenen Atmosphäre der reichen Vorkriegsgesellschaft, seinen bei aller Typisierung überzeugenden Menschen, seiner inquisitorischen Suche nach Wahrheit und Schuld, seiner unerbittlichen Folgerichtigkeit, seinen bitteren Ironien, seiner unerhörten Spannung und seiner eindringlich grimmigen Warnung«[21] gehört dieses Stück zum Besten, was Priestley geschrieben hat.

Berthold Sturm

20 Peinert, S. 338.
21 Löb, S. 67.

Inhalt

Reclams Rote Reihe

Reclam